THE GUNSMITH
#417 ACE HIGH

PRO SE PRESS

THE GUNSMITH #417: ACE HIGH
A Pro Se Press Publication

All rights reserved under U.S. and International copyright law. This book is licensed only for the private use of the purchaser. May not be copied, scanned, digitally reproduced, or printed for re-sale, may not be uploaded on shareware or free sites, or used in any other manner without the express written permission of the author and/or publisher. Thank you for respecting the hard work of the author.

THE GUNSMITH #417: ACE HIGH is a work of historical fiction. Many of the important historical events, figures, and locations are as accurately portrayed as possible. In keeping with a work of fiction, various events and occurrences were invented by the author.

Edited by Tommy Hancock
Editor in Chief, Pro Se Productions—Tommy Hancock
Submissions Editor—Rachel Lampi
Director of Corporate Operations—Kristi King-Morgan
Publisher & Pro Se Productions, LLC-Chief Executive Officer—Fuller Bumpers

Cover Art by Jeffrey Hayes
Print Production and Book Design by Percival Constantine
New Pulp Logo Design by Sean E. Ali
New Pulp Seal Design by Cari Reese

Pro Se Productions, LLC
133 1/2 Broad Street
Batesville, AR, 72501
870-834-4022

editorinchief@prose-press.com
www.prose-press.com

THE GUNSMITH #417: ACE HIGH

Published in digital form by Piccadilly Publishing,

THE GUNSMITH
#417 ACE HIGH

J.R. ROBERTS

PROSE PRESS

PROLOGUE

The Mississippi River

Henry Morgan walked the deck of the Natchez Queen, listening to the strains of music coming from the gambling hall. There was music, all right, from the piano player he had hired, but not much gambling going on. A few years ago the Queen would have been crowded with gamblers trying to get to the roulette wheel and poker tables. These days, not so much. The times that he'd pass the doors and hear the sound of that little white ball bouncing around on the wheel, or chips being tossed into the center of a table, were few and far between.

He shook his head, looked up at the bright moon, and headed for his cabin.

As he entered, his wife, Louisa, looked up from the writing desk he had bought her. Once she'd told him she wanted to travel the river with him and not stay at home in New Orleans waiting for his return, he did everything he could do to make her comfortable.

"Oh, there's that face," she said, putting down her quill.

"What face?" He walked to the sideboard and poured himself a brandy. He didn't offer her one. She was six months pregnant and determined to keep her body pure.

Louisa was five years younger than his 35, tall and

honey-haired, slender and beautiful. What she saw in him he would never know. There were rich men in New Orleans trying to win her hand but, at the late age of twenty-seven, she had chosen him to marry. She told him it was when she first saw him that she made up her mind. Her family had been worried, once she'd passed 25 without marrying, that she would end up an old maid, but she was bound and determined not to marry until she found the right man.

And that man was Henry Morgan.

Sometimes he wondered if it had simply been because he was a riverboat captain, and shared a name with the famed pirate, Captain Henry Morgan.

"What face?" he asked, again.

"That sad, sad expression I never want our baby to see on his father's handsome face."

Morgan knew he was anything but handsome. He had a scar that went from his right eyebrow, across his face, to the left corner of his mouth. He'd earned it in a knife fight during his first year on the river. She said it made him look distinguished.

"I'm sorry, my sweet," he said. "I was just walking around the deck—"

"—brooding about how nobody is on board, gambling."

"You know me too well." He put his hand on his shoulder and leaned over to kiss her.

"Look how handsome you are in your suit, and you're ruinin' it with that face you're makin'. Smile, my darling, and put your hand on my belly."

He smiled and did as she told him. Almost immediately he felt his son kick. He was convinced the baby was a boy, and would hear nothing to the contrary.

"There, see? He's happy to see you."

J.R. ROBERTS

"And I'm happy to see the both of you," he said, standing.

"Henry," she said, "you have a plan. Don't be so sad until you see how the plan works."

"If he comes."

"He said he'd come."

"It was just a telegram," he said. "What if we pull into Natchez tomorrow and he's not there..."

"He will be there, my love," she told him. "You said he was your friend."

"He is my friend," Henry said. "He saved my life, but that was several years ago."

"Friendship doesn't go away after a few years," she said. "Now, help me to my feet. We'll go and have our dinner."

"I'll have something brought here."

"Nonsense," she said. "We do have some passengers, and we want them to see their Captain enjoyin' his dinner."

He put his glass down and used both hands to assist her to her feet.

"Now hand me my wrap."

"Yes, Ma'am."

He grabbed the wrap from the back of another chair and placed it around her shoulders.

She kissed him and said, "I'm starved, and may I remind you I'm eatin' for two."

"Of course," he said. "Come on. We'll have the cook whip up something special."

As they started for the door there was a knock. Louisa's shoulders instantly slumped.

"Cap'n?" a voice called.

He looked at her and said, "I'm sorry, love."

"You better answer it."

THE GUNSMITH #417 - ACE HIGH

Henry walked to the door and opened it. His first mate, Byron Stanhope, filled the doorway in only the way a man six-foot-six could.

"What is it this time?"

"We got a problem, Cap'n." He looked past Henry at Louisa. "I'm sorry, my lady."

She'd told him time after time not to call her that, but he was a Brit, and there was nothing she could do to break him of the habit.

"Never mind," she said, removing her wrap. "I suppose I'll have my dinner in our cabin, after all."

"I'll have something brought up right away, my love," Henry said.

He kissed her and she playfully placed her hand on his cheek and pushed him away.

"Go, tend to your ship—my rival!"

"You have no rival, and know it."

"Cap'n?" Stanhope said, his tone concerned.

"I'm coming, Byron!"

As her husband followed his first mate out the door, their baby once again kicked her, only harder, this time.

"Oh yes, darlin'," she said, cradling her belly, "I know just how you feel."

ONE

Clint Adams arrived in Natchez, Mississippi well before the Natchez Queen Riverboat docked. The telegram he'd received from his friend, Henty Morgan, asked that he be in Natchez on May 5th, which he was. But there was no sign of Morgan's riverboat, the Natchez Queen. So he consigned Eclipse, his Darley Arabian, to a livery stable and got himself a room at the Natchez Grand Hotel.

On the first night he had supper in the hotel's dining room, which apparently catered not only to guests, but to the higher class citizens of Natchez. All around him were tables filled with couples of all ages; men dining together for business or personal reasons, and husbands and wives. All seemed to be enjoying their food—and company—very much. In fact, only two tables had less than two people seated at them—his, and one other.

At that table sat a woman with an admirable appetite. She had ordered a chicken dinner which, when delivered, took two waiters to carry. Clint was so impressed that he ordered the same. But as he worked his way through the meal, he noticed how she ate with much more gusto than he did. Although every inch a lady in her dress and actions, she consumed her food with mannish vigor. He found it fascinating to watch, and when she looked up and caught him watching, he could only smile and hope

THE GUNSMITH #417 - ACE HIGH

she would not be insulted—or worse yet, make a scene. However, all she did was smile back.

For the rest of the meal he tried not to be so obvious about watching her, but he'd never seen a woman eat with such fervor before. He thought he had succeeded in hiding his interest, with his waiter came over and said, "Sir, the lady would like to know if you would join her for dessert?"

"The lady?"

The waiter inclined his head and said, "The lady dining alone, sir."

He looked over and saw the woman he'd been watching smiling at him.

"Tell the lady I'd be—you know what? I'll tell her myself." He stood up. "Oh, and when we're finished, please being me my check, and the lady's."

"Very good, sir."

Clint walked over and stopped in front of the woman's table.

"Clint Adams," he said.

"Charlotte Chandler," she said, with a smile. "Please, sit."

Clint pulled out the chair across from her and sat. Up close she looked a little older than he had first thought, perhaps over thirty. She had dark hair, very pale skin, a slight double chin. She was lovely and, beneath the dress that covered her to the neck, a healthy girl.

"I saw you watching me eat," she said.

"You have an impressive appetite."

She smiled again. "As you can see, I'm a big girl."

"You're beautiful."

"Thank you," she said.

The waiter came and interrupted them.

"Dessert, Ma'am? Sir?"

6

"Apple pie for me," she said.

"Peach for me," Clint said.

"Coming up," the waiter said with a bow. "Coffee?"

"Yes," she said.

"Please," Clint said.

He backed away.

"So tell me," she said, "was my appetite the only reason you were watching me?"

"I'm sure you're used to men watching you."

"Not really," she said. "As I said, I'm a big girl. Most men like skinny women."

"Any man who wouldn't look at you is a fool."

"I thank you for that," she said, "and for keeping me company over dessert."

"Do you often eat alone?"

"I almost always eat alone," she said. "And you?"

"Often," he said. "I spend a lot of time alone on the trail."

"Do you get lonely?"

"Sometimes," he said, "but most of the times I find it...peaceful."

"And what brings you to a noisy, busy place like Natchez?"

"I'm meeting a friend of mine," he said.

The waiter came, set down their slices of pie, and coffee, then withdrew.

"When is that?" she asked.

"It was supposed to be today," he said, as they both picked up their forks, "but apparently he's not here yet."

"Lucky for me, then," she said. "I get to enjoy the pleasure of your company."

He smiled and said, "I think the pleasure is all mine."

TWO

Actually, the pleasure was both of theirs.

While they ate their pie, they got to know each other. As it turned out, they had both only just arrived in Natchez, and were waiting for the same boat.

"I've traveled a long way, from the East, to ride on a riverboat before they're all gone," she told him. "Why are you waiting for the Natchez Queen?"

"I told you, a friend of mine asked me to meet him here," Clint said. "He happens to own the Queen."

"Really?" she asked, excitedly.

"But I think he might be in trouble."

"And he asked you for help? Do your friends always ask you for help?"

He laughed shortly and said, "Very often."

"Then you must be a good man." she said, "a man who helps his friends is a good man."

"I suppose."

"No, you don't suppose," she said, "you know. She smiled. "I'll bet you get into more trouble helping other people."

"I've had my share."

When the waiter came with their checks, Clint convinced Charlotte to allow him to pay for her meal.

"Do you have a room here?" he asked, as they stepped into the lobby.

"I do."

"Can I walk you there? Or would you prefer a walk in the night air?"

"I think a walk to my room will do just fine," she said. "I can have a look at Natchez tomorrow."

As they strolled through the lobby, she drew looks from people there. She was almost as tall as Clint, and a solidly built lady. Her long dark hair and pale skin also attracted attention.

"Do you think the Natchez Queen will arrive tomorrow?" she asked him.

"I hope so," he said. "It was supposed to be here today. I'm hoping nothing's gone wrong."

"Would your friend have asked you to meet him here if everything was alright?"

"You have a point."

He walked her up the stairs to the second floor, up the hallway, past his own room to hers. When they got there she took her key from the small purse she was carrying and inserted it into the door, then turned to face him.

"Thank you for the company," she said, "and for the meal, and for seeing me to my room."

"You're welcome."

She leaned in to kiss him chastely on the cheek.

"I hope we'll both get to see the Natchez Queen tomorrow."

"Don't worry," he said. "Whenever it arrives, I'll take you aboard and introduce you to the owner."

"Oh, that would be wonderful," she said. She opened her door and said, "Good-night, Clint."

"Good-night, Charlotte."

She entered her room and closed the door. He heard the lock click into place, then walked back down the hall to his own room.

J.R. ROBERTS
***

As usual, Clint had a book in his saddlebags for his hotel stays. This time it was one of his friend Mark Twain's stories. THE PRINCE AND THE PAUPER.

He was sitting on the bed, boots off, his shirt unbuttoned but still on, and his gunbelt hanging on the bedpost, when there was a knock at the door. He slid the gun from the holster and walked across the room.

"Who is it?" he asked.

"The desk clerk, sir."

Holding the gun at his side he opened the door a crack with his left hand, saw the clerk standing there, and swung it wider. But he was still cautious in case someone was in the hall with the man. However, no one was.

"Yes, what is it?"

"I have a message for you, sir."

"I could have picked it up at the desk in the morning," Clint said.

"The lady asked me to deliver it right away, sir."

"The lady?"

"Yes, sir."

"All right, then. Deliver it."

"Yes, sir."

The clerk held a folded piece of paper out to him. He took it with his left hand, his right hand still at his side, holding his gun. The clerk noticed the weapon, and was properly nervous.

"Hold on, I'll get you someth—" Clint started.

"N-no, sir, that's fine," the clerk said. "All p-part of the service."

The clerk hurried back down the hall, almost running to the stairs.

Clint closed the door, walked to the bed and returned

THE GUNSMITH #417 - ACE HIGH

the gun to the holster. He unfolded the note and saw that it was from Charlotte Chandler.

It read: "I'm waiting!"

THREE

Clint quickly put his boots back onand, leaving his shirt unbuttoned, left his room and proceeded up the hall to Charlotte's door. When he reached it he saw that it was ajar, leaving no doubt as to what the message had meant.

He put his hand out pushed open the door. Charlotte turned, still wearing the same dress. She smiled at him, then frowned.

"Did you think you'd need your gun?"

He looked down at his sidearm.

"It goes with me everywhere."

"I see."

He closed the door behind him.

"I got your message," he said. "I hope I interpreted it right."

She approached him, put her hands inside his open shirt to touch his chest.

"I believe you did," she said, leaning in to kiss him.

Clint placed his hands on her waist, moved them down to her hips. He enjoyed how firm she felt beneath the dress.

"So you don't seem to mind a few extra pounds on a woman," she said.

"As a matter of fact," he said, "I prefer it."

"Well, that's fortunate, then."

THE GUNSMITH #417 - ACE HIGH

She backed away from him a few feet, reached behind her to undo her dress. Dropping the garment to the floor, she quickly did the same with her filmy underthings, until she stood there in front of him, gloriously naked.

Her breasts were like firm melons, with dark brown nipples, already distended. Her hips were wide, her belly convex, solid but not fat by any means. Between her full thighs was a forest of black pubic hair, something Clint liked very much. And she had beautifully shaped, solid calves. She was a living, breathing Rubens painting.

"You take my breath away," he said.

"I hope not," she replied. "I want to hear you say more nice things."

"I really don't want to talk," he said, approaching her. "I just want to act."

"That'll be good, too."

He paused long enough for her to remove his shirt and discard it, then put his arms around her and pulled her close. He kissed her, enjoying the way her breasts felt, mashed against his chest, so smooth and firm, with hard nipples.

Her tongue blossomed in his mouth and the kiss went on for a long time. He ran his hands down her back to her firm ass and clutched it.

She moaned into his mouth, writhed against him, then broke the kiss and asked, "Could we do away with the gun? And all these clothes?"

"I think that can be arranged," he said.

He unstrapped the gunbelt and hung it on the bedpost, while she pulled down the quilt. He stepped back to watch her bend over the bed to do it.

"What are you doing?" she asked, straightening.

"Just looking," he said. "You're...amazing."

She blushed and he found it hard to believe she didn't

receive such compliments all the time.

"Let me help you," she said, reaching for his belt. She undid it, unbuttoned his trousers, but before removing them, pushed him down on the bed so she could take off his boots. That done, he lifted his butt from the mattress so she could slide off his trousers and underwear. As she did that his hard cock sprang into view, and her eyes widened with delight.

"Oh, yes," she said, taking his erection in her hand, "I knew you would be a beautiful man."

"Now it's my turn to blush," he said, although he didn't.

"Nonsense," she said, "you've had many women, Clint Adams. If I didn't know your reputation, I'd know that much, anyway."

She got on her knees in front of him, ran her hands over his thighs, and then turned her attention back to his penis. With one hand she grasped and stroked it, while with the other she reached beneath and cupped his testicles.

He watched her as she gave her full attention to what she was doing. She looked very content, until she ducked her head so that he couldn't see her face. He felt her mouth, though, as she first wet the head of his cock with her tongue, and then took it inside. She sucked it, wetting it thoroughly, then slid her fingers down the shaft so that her lips could slide down after them.

He leaned back and closed his eyes as her head began to bob up and down. Then he decided he didn't want his eyes to be closed. Not while he could still see her beautiful hair, the smooth skin of her shoulders and back, the muscles in her forearms as she continued to use her fingers along with her lips and mouth.

He took her ministrations for as long as he could and

was about to pull her off when she released him from her mouth and raised her eyes to look at him.

"Come up here," he said, roughly. He reached down, took her beneath her arms, and pulled her onto the bed, where they fell together.

FOUR

There was not enough time in one night to explore all of Charlotte Chandler's curves.

But Clint Adams gave it a good try.

"Oh Lord," she said, waking to the sun coming through the window, and his face between her thighs, "you are insatiable."

"You're that kind of woman," he said. "Or didn't you know it?"

"What kind is that?"

"If a man is with you," he said, stroking her thigh, "he wants to do things to you. He can't help it."

He reached up with one hand to stroke a breast, a nipple, while he pressed his face to her again. She laughed, a throaty, happy sound, and reached down to hold his head in place.

He probed through the dark jungle of hair between her legs until he found her, wet and waiting for him already. With a stroke of his tongue he caused her to catch her breath. Thereafter, she was gasping for air as he urged her toward orgasm with his tongue and lips. Amazingly, she became more and more wet, until she was gushing, soaking his face and the bedsheets. Finally, she lifted her butt up off the bed and stifled a scream. He felt the tremors run through her belly. Before they could end, he lifted himself above her, pressed his hard cock to her wet pussy and plunged into her. This time the scream almost escaped her lips, but she turned her head and buried her face in the pillow.

He rode her, slamming in and out of her with unbridled fury as he sought his own release. She was big and solid enough to withstand it and, in fact, put her arms and legs around him so she could contribute to the force of the coupling. He didn't recall ever having a more powerful pair of legs wrapped around his waist.

The room quickly filled with the sound of their flesh slapping together, her cries and his grunts and then, when he couldn't hold back any longer, a long, guttural moan as he emptied his seed into her. Moments later she threw her head back and let out the scream she'd been holding in all night long...

***

They waited, lying together on the bed, to see if anyone would knock on the door, looking for the source of her scream.

"Maybe nobody heard me?" she said, hopefully.

"Maybe," he said, "I'm sure it's not the first time they've heard such a thing in this hotel."

She giggled, and buried her face in his bare shoulder. Moments later she began to nibble on him, working her way up to his neck, her hand moving down between his legs.

"Oh God," she said, pulling her hand away.

"What?"

"I expected to find you soft." She looked down at him. "We've been at it all night and you're still like that?"

"I told you, woman," he said, "it's your fault. And you're going to have to do something about it, because

J.R. ROBERTS

I can't sit and eat breakfast with this thing between my legs."

"Well," she said, "All right, but I warn you—" she slithered down between his legs and took hold of him, "—I tend to enjoy it."

As she took him into her hot, wet mouth, he said forcefully, "Me, too!"

***

Later they decided to have breakfast together. First he had to go back to his own room so they could both wash up, and put on fresh clothing. When he met her in the lobby she was wearing one of those day dresses that covered her from head to toe.

"Shall we eat?" she asked.

"Why not?" he asked. "I think we've both worked up an appetite, don't you?"

"You've got the nerve to ask me that?" she said. "I'm famished!"

They were seated in the dining room immediately, drawing looks from the other diners.

"See?" he said to her. "They're looking at you."

"They're looking at us," she corrected him. "We make a striking couple."

"Or they know it was you who screamed."

"Or," she shot back at him, "they know who you are."

"So you knew who I was when I introduced myself to you last night," he said.

"Well, I...yes," she said. "As soon as I heard your name."

"Why didn't you say anything?"

"Did you want me to say something?" she asked. "I thought you might like to have a nice evening without someone mentioning your reputation."

"Actually, you were right about that. And thank you."

"You're welcome."

A waiter came over to take their order, and quickly brought them a pot of coffee and two cups, then went off to get their food.

When he brought their food they started immediately eating, both with a lot of gusto and not much conversation. About halfway through they slowed down and looked at each other.

"Are you going to the docks this morning to see if the Natchez Queen has come in?"

"I am," he said. "Would you like to come along?"

"I'd love to," she said, "but do you think we could get some more ham?"

He smiled and said, "I'm sure of it," waving to the waiter.

FIVE

They walked together to the Natchez docks, strolling actually, in no particular hurry. She linked her arm through his right arm, but he moved her over to the left side.

"Ah," she said, "you have to keep your gun arm free, don't you?"

"Always."

"Even here?" she asked. "In Natchez?"

"Everywhere," he said. "It's the only way I stay alive. That, or stay off the streets, and I can't do that."

"You're not the kind of man to hide away, are you?" she asked.

"Not at all."

"So where do you spend most of your time?" she asked.

"On the trail," he said. "Sleeping under the stars."

"But obviously, you do get to towns and cities from time to time."

"Obviously?"

"Well," she said, "you're a man who knows how to be with a women. You can't learn that on the trail, can you?"

"No, you're right about that."

When they reached the docks it was busy, with several ships having apparently just come in. They were being unloaded, and others were being loaded, preparing to leave.

"Is it here?" she asked.

"I don't see it."

"It's so busy," she said. "Would you know it?"

"I've seen the Queen before, but it was several years ago. Come on, we'll walk around."

They started to walk, looking at the boats, and once or twice were warned away because they might get hurt.

"Do you know if the Natchez Queen has come in today?" Clint asked one of the longshoremen who was unloading.

"Natchez Queen? Never heard of it. Ask the Dockmaster. Now, get out of the way before somethin' falls on you."

***

After trying a bit longer and not finding the Natchez Queen on the docks, they went in search of the Dockmaster. They found a man in a small office who was very distracted with a lot of papers on his desk.

"The Natchez Queen was supposed to be in yesterday," he said, without looking at them.

"We know," Clint said. "I was supposed to meet it."

"Well," the man said, this time looking up, "it didn't come in." He started to look back down at his desk, but saw Charlotte and stopped. He was a man in his fifties, with a heavy beard and beady eyes, which he now couldn't take off of her.

"You, too?" he asked her.

"Yes," she said, "I'm, uh, waiting for the Natchez Queen also."

"Well," he said, "maybe it'll come in today. Do

you wanna wait here? I can get you a chair." He looked around desperately, "there's one here, somewhere."

"That's okay," Clint said, "we'll wait outside."

"She can wait here," the man said.

"No," she said, "I'll go outside with my friend."

"Uh, yeah, okay."

"Thanks for your help," Clint said.

They went back outside.

"I'll take you back to the hotel and then come back and wait a while."

"That's okay," she said. "You stay here. I can find my way back."

"Did you see the way the Dockmaster looked at you?"

She hesitated, then said, "Yes, okay, you can walk me back."

***

He entered the lobby with her and stopped.

"Going to your room?" he asked.

"Only if I can convince you to come with me," she said.

"It wouldn't take much convincing," he said, "but I have to get back to the docks."

"Then I think I'll do some shopping," she said. "Just for a little while."

"If the boat comes in, I'll let you know."

"And if not?"

"I'll come and take you to supper."

She smiled. "That's a deal. I know I'll be hungry by then."

"You're always hungry."

"Lucky for you, you like big girls."

He kissed her and whispered, "I love big girls. I'll see you later."

He left the hotel and started walking back to the docks.

***

The four men watched him leave the hotel.

"We should have stopped them together," one of them said.

"We were told to stop him," another said, "not the woman."

"I ain't attackin' no woman," a third said.

"No," the fourth man said, "we ain't. We're just gonna do what we was paid to do. Come on."

They started off after Clint Adams.

SIX

Clint blamed his own stupidity.

Afterward he realized that another careless incident like this one could cost him his life. Was he getting old? Too old to be the Gunsmith, with a permanent bullseye on his back? Maybe he should go into hiding on a small ranch somewhere in Idaho, or some other, out of the way place. The Southern part of Mexico? Maybe a beach on the Gulf?

But all that introspection came later...

He was walking quickly back to the docks. The men following knew where he was going, and knew a short cut. When he came to the dirty, weather-cracked streets that led directly to the waterfront, they pounced.

There were four, armed with knives. One of them simply leaped from cover, and collided with Clint, taking him off his feet. They had instructions not to let him get to his gun.

As Clint went down in the street he tried to roll, but the other three men were good at this. They often attacked men in the street with the aim of robbing them. This was a little different, though.

One of them had a pistol, but he was told not to use it unless it was absolutely necessary. The aim was not to kill the Gunsmith, just to keep him from making it back to the docks to meet the Natchez Queen as it came in.

THE GUNSMITH #417 - ACE HIGH

Clint felt his arms gripped immediately, as he was hauled to his feet. Then someone plucked his gun from his holster and tossed it away.

It got quiet.

Some passersbys crossed to the other side of the street and hurried along. They were used to this, and knew not to get involved.

"What's this about?" Clint asked.

"Nothin' personal," said the man standing directly in front of him. The men on either side held his arms, and the fourth man stood off to one side, presumably keeping watch.

The man in front of him swung, hitting him in the stomach. The air went out of his lungs, but the two men holding him kept him from doubling over.

"Come on," said the man on watch, "get on with it before someone calls the law."

"Down here?" the first man asked. "What are the chances?"

"Things are changin'," said the fourth man.

The first man hit Clint again in the stomach. Clint deliberately went slack so the two men holding him would think they had to support him up. As they shifted their hands to put them beneath his armpits they relaxed their hold on his arms. He yanked himself free and launched a kick into the stomach of the man who had hit him.

The man on watch turned and widened his eyes as he saw what was going on.

"Damn it, grab him!" he shouted.

Before either man could do that, Clint turned and hit one on the jaw. As the other tried to grab him from behind he turned quickly, put both hands against his chest and pushed violently. The man stumbled back, struck the front window of an empty shop, and tumbled through with a loud shattering of the glass.

Clint turned his attention to the man he had kicked, who was down on one knee. Rather than trying to get to his feet, he seemed to be reaching for something in his belt.

Clint moved in closer just as the man brought a gun out. Clint kicked again, and the gun went spinning from the man's hand. He kicked a third time, catching the man under the chin.

When he turned to face the fourth man, he saw that he had taken off running. The other men were scrambling to their feet, one of them climbing out through the broken window. They also ran.

He turned to the man who had hit him. He was on his back in the street, not unconscious but dazed. That gave Clint time to look around and find his gun. It would need cleaning, but for now he blew on it, and slid it back into his holster.

He walked to the fallen man as he was propping himself up on his elbows. He looked up at Clint and his eyes widened.

"Don't kill me," he said.

"Why not? Weren't you going to kill me?"

"No!" the man snapped. "No, we weren't. We were only supposed to..."

"To what?"

"Rough you up," the man said. "Keep you from gettin' to the dock this mornin'."

"Why?"

"I don't know."

"Who hired you?"

"I don't know."

Clint reached out and grabbed a handful of the man's shirt.

"I swear," he said. "It was one of the others who got the job."

"It seemed to me you were in charge."

"I'm the muscle," he said. "The man on watch, he was in charge."

"What's your name?"

"Gage."

"And what's his name?"

"Barrow."

"Where can I find him?"

"He lives in a hotel down here, near the docks. It's called The River Hotel."

"Do you live there?"

"No, I live somewhere else."

Clint released his shirt and stood up.

"Get going."

The man staggered to his feet.

"You're not gonna kill me?"

"Not now," Clint said, "but if I see you again..."

"You won't," Gage said, backing away, "you won't, I swear." He turned and ran.

Clint found his hat, took a moment to collect his wits and rub his stomach, where he had been hit twice, then continued on his way to the docks.

SEVEN

When Clint reached the docks, they were even busier than when he was there last. Instead of looking around for the Natchez Queen this time, however, he went directly to the Dockmaster's office, climbed the steps and entered.

The man looked up as Clint entered, then looked past him. A disappointed expression came over his face.

"Where's the lady?" he asked.

"Never mind," Clint said. "Did the Natchez Queen come in?"

"Yeah, yeah," the man said, "it just docked now. Look."

He took Clint to a window and pointed. Clint saw a paddlewheel riverboat with the named NATCHEZ QUEEN written along the side.

"There she is," the man said.

"Any problem with me going down there?"

"Nah, go ahead, if you want," the man said. "So, that lady's not here with you?"

"No, not this time."

"What you got going on with the Natchez Queen?" the Dock Master asked.

"The owner's a friend of mine."

"Oh."

"Okay, thanks."

THE GUNSMITH #417 - ACE HIGH

"Yeah."

The man went back to his desk, and Clint left the office.

***

"I've got to go ashore," Henry Morgan told his wife.

"What about the repairs?"

"Byron is overseeing them," Morgan said. "Now that we're docked we'll be able to get all the parts we need."

"And the guests?"

"They can come or go as they please," Morgan said. "But they better be back before we shove off again."

She looked up from her paperwork. She kept the books for their business.

"Do you want to go ashore?" he asked her.

"No," she said, "I have things to do."

"I'll be back soon."

"Are you going to look for Clint Adams?"

"I'll keep my eye out," he said. "I'm hopin' he'll come lookin' for us, though."

She stood up and put her hands on her husband's chest.

"Whatever happens," she said, "I know you'll figure it out. I believe in you."

He kissed her, then hugged her tightly.

"I'll see you in a little while," he promised, and left the cabin.

***

He found his first mate out on the deck.

"What's goin' on, Byron?" he asked.

"We're gettin' the parts we need," Byron replied.

"Are we gonna be ready to go?"

"We are," Byron said, "if we don't get sabotaged, again."

"We'll keep up the guard schedule we implemented and hope that doesn't happen."

"Aye, sir, we will."

Morgan slapped Byron Stanhope on his big shoulder and said, "I'll be back, soon."

"We'll be ready."

Morgan nodded, then went down the gangplank to the dock.

***

Clint thought he knew exactly where the Natchez Queen was, but when he left the Dockmaster's office he got lost. It seemed it took him an hour to find it, but it was only about ten minutes. However, it was ten minutes of ducking longshoremen, and crates that were being loaded or unloaded.

Finally, he found himself standing alongside the boat, and took a moment to admire it. He'd seen it years ago, when Henry Morgan had first bought it. For some reason, it looked bigger to him now.

Eventually—after evading a few more crates and longshoremen—he made his way up the gangplank, only to have his path blocked by a large man at the top.

"Can I help ya?" the man asked.

"I'm looking for Henry Morgan."

"Why?"

"Why are you asking?" Clint asked, irked by the man's attitude.

"Because I'm the first mate," the man said. "You wanna see the Cap'n, you go through me, first."

Clint had heard the same thing from many foremen

on many ranches. Some authority just seemed to go to people's heads.

"He's a friend of mine."

"That so?" Byron asked. "And what's your name?"

"Clint Adams."

The man didn't react beyond a sudden relaxing of his body.

"Oh," he said, backing away so that he was no longer blocking Clint's way. "Right. I'm Byron Stanhope, the first mate."

Clint stepped off the gangplank up onto the deck. The two men faced each other, unsure of what to do. Finally, Clint put out his hand, and Stanhope shook it.

"Is he here?" Clint asked. "Henry?"

"You just missed him," Stanhope said. "He had to go ashore."

"Oh," Clint said, "that's too bad."

"Watch it!" somebody behind him yelled.

Clint stepped aside and a longshoreman came through, carrying a crate.

"Are you carrying...cargo?" Clint asked. "I thought the point of the Natchez Queen was gambling?"

"No, not cargo," Bryon said, "those are parts."

"Oh," Clint said, "for...repairs?"

"That's right."

When Stanhope wasn't very forthcoming, Clint thought he got the idea.

"Is there a problem?" Clint asked. "When I got the telegram from Henry he only asked me to meet him here, but didn't say—"

"Maybe," Stanhope said, "you better talk to Louisa."

"Louisa?"

"The Cap'n's wife."

"Henry's married?"

"Well, yeah," Stanhope said. "There's more, but you better hear it from her."

"Okay, but—"

"Come this way."

EIGHT

"Byron!" The woman who answered the door looked surprised. "Is there a problem?"

"No, Milady, no problem," Stanhope said, "but the Cap'n's friend is here."

"His friend?" "Clint Adams?"

"Oh! Where is he?"

Stanhope waved and Clint came from down the hall, where he'd been waiting.

"Mr. Adams, this is Louisa Morgan."

"Clint! It's so good to meet you."

"You, too, Louisa."

"Please, come in," she said. "I'm sorry Henry's not here. Did Byron tell you?"

"Yes, he did."

"And I have to go back on deck and oversee the repairs," Byron said.

"Go ahead," Louisa said. "I'll entertain Clint until Henry gets back."

"Yes, Milday."

After Byron left Clint asked, "Why does he call you 'Milady?'"

"He's British," she said. "Apparently, that's what they do."

Clint looked around the cabin, which was small and

THE GUNSMITH #417 - ACE HIGH

neat. There was an open doorway to another room, where he saw a bed.

"Would you like a drink?" she asked. "We have some brandy, and whiskey."

"I will if you will."

"Oh, not for me," she said.

"You don't drink?"

"I do," she said, "but I don't think it's wise, right now." She touched her stomach. "I'm pregnant."

"Pregnant!" Clint said. "So that's what Stanhope meant when he said there was more. I didn't even know Henry had gotten married. That's great! I mean, great that your married, and that you're pregnant."

"Thank you," she said. "I can get someone from the galley to bring up some coffee."

"Coffee would be good," he said.

"And then we can sit and get to know each other until Henry gets back," she said, "which should be soon."

"Where did he go, exactly?"

"He didn't say," she said. "Just that he had something to do. I'll be right back. Have a seat."

She left the cabin and he sat at the small, round table which looked as if it served a lot of uses—a dinner table, a desk, whatever.

As he looked around, Clint had the feeling he was seeing where his friend, Henry Morgan, had been living during the intervening years since they'd last seen each other. It was small, especially for two people. Or perhaps Henry and his wife, Louisa, liked it this way.

Louisa returned and smiled.

"We'll have coffee and something to eat soon," she said. "Please, don't stand on my account."

"I won't, if you will sit," he said.

"I will," she said, and did. She rested her hands in her

lap, very near to her protruding belly. "Henry will be so glad you're here."

"I was here yesterday, when he said you'd be getting in," Clint said.

"We were unavoidably detained."

"By what?"

"I should let Henry tell you."

Clint leaned forward.

"But you can tell me, can't you?"

She placed her hands over her stomach, then looked at him and said, "Sabotage!"

He saw the tears in her eyes and knew how serious she was.

"How long has it been going on?"

"Since we left New Orleans," she said. "Business has been bad all on its own accord, but when things started to go wrong...it just got worse. Some people canceled their bookings, said they didn't want to be on a boat that was...jinxed."

"Jinxed?" Clint repeated. "That's ridiculous."

"I agree."

"Does Henry have any idea who's behind it?"

"No," she said. "He's afraid it's one of the crew."

"One of his own men?"

She nodded.

"It breaks his heart to think so, but yes." She shook her head. "Poor Henry."

"So he sent for me to help?"

"He sent for you on another matter," she said. "But perhaps you can help while you're here. That is, if you agree to this other matter."

"Which is?"

"Now that. I will let him tell you," she said. There was a knock at the door. "That will be our coffee and food."

"I'll get it," he said. "You sit."

He walked to the door and opened it. A young man holding a tray looked surprised to see him.

"It's all right, Alfred," Louisa said. "Bring it in and put it on the table."

"Yes, Ma'am."

The young man carried the tray in, set it down and then smiled at Louisa. Clint could tell from the look on his face that he adored her.

"This is Mr. Adams, a friend of the Captain's."

"Yes, Ma'am." The young man looked at Clint. "Hello."

Clint nodded.

"Can I get you anything else, Miss Louisa?" he asked.

"No, Alfred," she said. "That'll be all. You can go."

"Yes, Ma'am."

The young man left and Clint closed the door behind him.

"You know he's in love with you," he said, sitting back down.

"He's impressionable," she said. "Shall I pour?"

"Please."

NINE

They drank coffee and ate cake which Louisa said he had been prepared by their own cook.

"This is very good," Clint said.

"Wait until you feast on his regular cooking," she said. "Breakfast, and supper."

"Then your passengers are eating well."

"Oh, yes," she said. "So far the galley hasn't been sabotaged."

"That's good."

"Just the paddlewheel, the boiler, the hull," she said, bitterly. "Nothing important, right?"

"So things have been rough."

"The roughest," she said. "We barely limped into port here."

"Which is why I saw parts being brought on board."

"Yes."

"Then the repairs are being made even now."

"With Byron's supervision."

"So what took Henry ashore?"

"You'll have to ask him that when he returns," she said. "Which should be any time now."

"I'll wait."

"I hope you'll do more than that."

"How do you mean?"

"I know he wants you to be with us when we shove

THE GUNSMITH #417 - ACE HIGH

off again," she said. "I can have you taken to your cabin."

"I'd have to go back to my hotel and get my things," he said, "and take care of my horse."

"Would you want to take him with you?" she asked. "We can accommodate him."

"That's a thought," Clint said. "I'd hate to leave him behind."

"Then it's done."

"If I agree to go," Clint said. "Also, I met a woman who wants to buy passage on board. Do you have room?"

"Plenty," she said. "We're nowhere near full."

"Then I'll go back to my hotel, fetch her, and my things," Clint said. "If you and Henry need my help, I'll come along."

"I suppose," she said, "before you make your final decision you should talk with Henry, hear what he was originally going to ask you to do for him."

"Is it something I won't want to do?" he asked.

"I...don't know."

He was in the act of standing. Instead, he settled back into his chair.

"Then I guess I'd better wait for Henry and find out what's going on," Clint said.

"More coffee, then?"

"Why not?"

***

Bryon Stanhope was watching the repairs on the paddlewheel when a crewman came up behind him.

"Sir, you wanted to know when the Cap'n was back?"

"That's right."

"He's comin' up the gangway now."

"Thank you." He turned to the men working on the

wheel. "Keep goin'. I'll be back."

"Yessir!"

Stanhope turned and walked to intercept Captain Morgan.

***

Morgan came off the gangway and saw his first mate striding toward him purposefully.

"Don't give me any bad news, Byron," he said. "I've had enough for one day."

"Not bad news, Cap'n," Stanhope said. "Your friend is here."

"Friend?"

"Clint Adams."

"Clint's here? Where?"

"I took him to see Milady Louisa," Stanhope said.

"Good, good," Morgan said. "This could turn the tide, Byron."

"I don't see how, Cap'n."

"You will, Byron," Morgan said, "you will."

TEN

"Clint!" Morgan shouted, exploding into the room.

"Henry!" Clint stood up and the younger man embraced him.

Clint looked at the smiling Louisa and said, "It's been a long time since I was hugged by a Captain."

"I told her you'd come," Morgan said.

"And here I am," Clint said. "Your bride has been keeping me occupied."

"And did she tell you I'm to be a father?"

"She did! That's wonderful."

"Is that coffee and cake? I'm famished."

"Then sit, my love," Louisa said. "I'll pour, and you and Clint can catch up."

Henry sat and Louisa poured them each a cup of coffee.

"Have some cake," she said, "and I'll go into the bedroom for a nap. I'm quite tired."

"Forgive me," Clint said, "I've tired you out."

"Nonsense," she said, "it's Henry's son who has tired me out with his kicking."

"Son?" Clint asked.

"But of course," Morgan said. "What else would it be?"

"I'll see you both later."

She kissed her husband and went into the bedroom,

closing the door behind her.

Henry Morgan picked up a piece of cake and bit into it.

"How much did Louisa tell you?"

"She told me about sabotage," Clint said. "That's all. She said there was more, but that you'd tell me. She's a fine woman."

"She's wonderful," Morgan said. "She's stood by me through all of this."

"And why wouldn't she?" Clint asked. "She's your wife."

"Yes," he said, "and I'm a lucky man for it."

"I'll help in any way I can, Henry," Clint said, "but the sabotage is not really why you sent for me."

"No, it's not," Morgan said. "I've heard stories about you, Clint."

"There are a lot of them," Clint said. "Which ones are you talking about?"

"Your poker playing."

"Oh, that," Clint said. "It's the least of my talents."

"That's not what I've heard," Morgan said. "They say you've played with the best—Bat Masterson, Doc Holliday, the brothers Brett and Bart, even that fella Hawkes."

"I have," Clint said. "And I've lost a lot of my money to them. But tell me, what's the problem, Henry?"

"Okay, but first, do you want somethin' to drink other than coffee?"

"Your wife offered me some kind of brandy, I think," Clint said, "and whiskey. I thanked her, but said I didn't want—"

"No," Henry said, "I'm talkin' about somethin' else."

"What is it?"

"You'll see."

J.R. ROBERTS

"When?"

There was a knock on the door at that moment.

"That should be it. I told Byron to wait a short while, and then bring it up."

Henry Morgan walked to the door and opened it.

"Thanks, Byron." He took what the first mate handed him, then closed the door without inviting the man in. He turned and carried it to the table, setting it down in the center.

"What is it?" Clint asked.

"What's it look like?"

"A pail."

"That's what it is," Henry said. "A pail of beer."

"Beer? From where?"

"From the hold of this ship." Henry hurried to the little sidebar for two glasses, brought them back to the table. He carefully poured some beer from the pail into the glass.

"I got a great cook on my boat, Clint, but he also brews his own beer—and this is it. Have a taste."

Clint lifted his glass, looked doubtfully at the murky color, but then took a taste, and then another.

"Well?" Henry asked.

"It's good," Clint said. "It's real good."

"I knew you'd like it!" Henry clinked glasses with Clint and they both drank the beer down.

"More?" Henry asked.

"We can have some more later. What I need right now is for you to have a seat and tell me why you asked me to meet you here."

Henry's shoulders slumped. He put his glass down and sat.

"I could lose my boat, Clint," he said. I could lose he Natchez Queen."

"Because of the sabotage?"

"Partly," Henry said. "Business has just been really bad, Clint. I had to do somethin'!"

"So you asked me to come."

"Yes."

"So what is it you want me to do, Henry?"

Henry stared at Clint for a moment, then said, "I want you to play poker."

***

The cook, Terry Robespierre, from New Orleans, was waiting for the first mate when he came up.

"Did he do it?" he asked. "Did the Captain give my beer to Clint Adams to taste?"

"I don't know, Terry."

"But...didn't you bring it up?"

"I did, and the Cap'n took it from me at the door."

The young cook asked, "He didn't invite you in?"

"No," Byron said, "I guess the boss figures the beer was just for him and the Gunsmith?"

"Well, is he gon' be with us the rest of the way upriver?" the cook asked.

"I don't know, Terry," Byron said. "I guess we'll all just have to wait and find out."

"But...you're the first mate."

"And I've got work to do," Byron said. "And by the way, so do you."

"But Byron—"

"Get to it!" Byron said, and continued along the deck.

***

"You want me to play poker?"

"Yes, I do," Henry said. "And I want to let it be

J.R. ROBERTS

known that the Gunsmith will be playin' poker on the Natchez Queen."

Clint looked surprised.

"You want to advertise?"

"Yes," Henry said, "Well no, not when you put it that way. I just want to...let the word get around."

"And you think this will fix your business, Henry?" Clint asked.

"I think it will bring me more passengers," Henry said.

"You're putting a lot of faith in people wanting to play poker against me."

"Or just wantin' to watch you."

Clint thought this over for a moment or two.

"How long would you want me to do this?" he asked.

"Once or twice up and down the river Clint," Henry said. "That's it. By then I'll know for sure whether or not I'm losin' the boat."

"Henry, there must be more to this than just filling the boat with passengers."

"Some," Henry said, "But for now this is all I'm willin' to ask of you. I need his, Clint, for my wife, and my baby."

Clint thought again, rubbed the back of his neck, then said, "Ah, what the hell. Let's do it."

"Really?" Henry Morgan asked, excitedly.

"Really," Clint said, "but pour me another glass of that beer before it gets warm."

ELEVEN

"I can take you around and introduce you to the other members of the crew."

"How are they going to feel about me being here?" he asked.

"They can feel whatever they want to feel," Henry said. "It's my boat."

"Yeah, but if you've got gambling on your boat, that means you've got dealers."

"They'll still be dealin'. You're gonna have your own table."

"Henry," Clint said, "you're buying yourself a lot of trouble."

"I already have a lot of trouble, Clint."

"I tell you what," Clint said. "I'll go to my hotel and pick up my things. I also have a guest I'll be bringing back with me."

"A guest?"

"A lady," Clint said. "She's from back East, and has come all this way to ride on a Mississippi riverboat."

"She's welcome."

"While I'm gone," Clint said, "talk to your people. Make it sound like you're clearing it with them for me to play on board."

"That's not the way I run my business, Clint," Henry said.

THE GUNSMITH #417 - ACE HIGH

"Henry, it sounds to me like you're having some trouble running your business the way you usually work."

A muscle jumped in Captain Morgan's jaw, but then it relaxed and he said, "You're probably right."

"Then we're agreed?"

Henry nodded. "Agreed."

The two friends finished their beer, stood up and shook hands.

"And one other thing," Clint said.

"What's that?"

"I think you should have invited your first mate in on this meeting," Clint said. "And let him have a beer with us."

"Byron knows his job, Clint," Henry said, "and his place. I'm not going to apologize to him. He would think it strange."

"All right," Clint said. "He's your first mate. You probably know best how to treat him."

"Let me walk you ashore," Henry said, and the two men left the cabin.

***

Byron Stanhope and several other members of the crew watched as Henry Morgan walked Clint off the Natchez Queen. Once on the dock, the two men shook hands again.

"What's goin' on, First Nate?" a crewman asked.

"You'll find out when the Captain wants to tell ya," Byron said. "Now get back to work."

"Yessir."

Byron went to meet his Captain as he came back aboard.

"So?" he asked. "Is he gonna do it?"

"He is."

"Did you tell him everythin'?"

"Not quite."

"When will you?"

"Once we're under way," Henry said, "and he can't get off without swimmin' back to shore. Besides, he's bringin' a guest, and his horse."

"A horse? On board."

"That's right," Henry said. "Make room for it."

"Yes, sir. And his guest."

"It's a woman," Henry said. "and if Clint is still the same ol' Clint, I think she'll be sharin' his cabin—but have one prepared for her, anyway."

"Yessir."

As the first mate started to turn away, Henry said, "Oh, and Byron."

"Yessir?"

"I should have invited you in to have a beer with us." That was all he said, not considering it to have been an apology.

Byron Stanhope looked at him funny and said, "Yessir," and then continued away.

***

When Henry entered his cabin, his wife, Louisa, was awake and waiting for him.

"Is he going to do it?" she asked.

"Yes, he is." He went to her and hugged her.

"Did you tell him everything?"

"No," Henry said, "not quite everythin', my love."

She stepped away, but only so she could look him in the face, and not outside the circle of his arms.

"Don't you think you should have?"

"Yes," he said, pulling her close again, "I probably should have."

TWELVE

When Clint got back to his hotel he stopped at Charlotte's room.

"Are you ready to go?" he asked, when she opened the door.

She smiled happily and asked, "The boat's here?"

"It is?"

"And it's all arranged?"

"Yes, it's arranged. If you need time to pack—"

She stepped back so he could look into the room and said, "I'm packed!"

He saw several pieces of luggage in the center of the room, including a trunk.

"All that?" he asked.

"I'm not the kind of girl who travels light, Clint Adams."

"No," he said, "obviously you are not. I'll, uh, have to go get some help to load your things onto a buckboard. And I'll, uh, have to rent a buckboard."

"I can pay for it!" she offered.

"That's not a problem," he assured her. "I'll be back as shortly."

***

When the buckboard was fully loaded, Clint paid the

two men he'd found to help, lifting Charlotte up onto the sea. He joined her there, then picked up the reins. Eclipse was loosely tethered to the rear, just to let him know which way they were going.

"This is so exciting," Charlotte said, leaning against him. "What was it your friend, the Captain, wants you to do?"

"Not much," he said. "Just play poker."

"Play cards? Why?"

"He's having some trouble getting passengers."

"And he thinks people will ride his boat to play cards with you?"

"Not cards," Clint corrected her. "Poker."

"Is there a difference?"

"Do you play cards?"

"I've played bridge," she said. "I'm not very good at it. Is it like that?"

"Not at all."

"How is it different?"

"Well, for one thing, there's usually money on the table."

"A lot of money?"

"Sometimes."

"And you're good at it?"

"Fairly good."

"So people will pay to come on board and lose to you?"

"That's what Captain Morgan figures."

She shook her head. "I'm afraid it makes no sense to me."

"Maybe Henry's wife can explain it to you."

"Wait," she said, "His name's Henry *Morgan*?" she asked. "Like the pirate?"

"Exactly like the pirate."

"And it's his real name?"
"As far as I know."
"That's amazing."
"One more thing."
"What?"
"His wife is pregnant."
"How wonderful!" she said. "Is it their first?"
"Yes."
"But wait...is she on the boat?"
"She is."
"Pregnant?"
"Yes."
"They live on the boat?"
"For now."
She shook her head again,
"This is going to be a very interesting trip on the Mississippi, indeed."

***

Clint was surprised to see, when they arrived at the dock, there were men not only to take Charlotte's luggage aboard, but Eclipse, as well.

"You'll have to be careful with him," Clint told the man who was in charge of Eclipse.

Oh, I'll be careful with him all right, sir," the crewman said. "What a magnificent beast!"

Clint saw where the man was looking and wasn't at all sure he was talking about the Darley Arabian.

"No," he said, "you're not listening."

"Sir?" the man asked.

"I didn't say you have to be careful with him, I said you have to be careful of him."

"How's that, sir?"

THE GUNSMITH #417 - ACE HIGH

"He might take a finger off!"

THIRTEEN

Clint took Charlotte to Henry Morgan's cabin and introduced her to the Captain and his wife, Louisa.

"Any guest of Clint's is a guest of ours," Louisa said. "Welcome aboard."

"Thank you so much," Charlotte said, "but it is my intention to pay my own way."

"Nonsense," Henry said. "That's not what the word 'guest' means."

"Well—"

"We'll hear no more talk of it," Louisa said. "Come with me and I'll show you to your cabin. I assume you want your own?"

"Well, of course..."

"Then come this way," the Captain's wife said, taking Charlotte's arm.

As they walked out the door, Clint heard Charlotte say, "I understand you're pregnant. How wonderful! You must be so excited..."

The ladies closed the door behind them.

"Thanks for that," Clint said.

"I'm the one who should do the thankin'," Henry said.

"When do we shove off?" Clint asked.

"You've been on riverboats before," Henry said, "haven't you?"

"Yes, many years ago. I was on one with Sam Clemens once, but that's a long story."

"On a riverboat with Mark Twain?" Henry asked. "You're gonna have to tell me that one."

"One of these days," Clint said. "How about it? When do we leave?"

"I'll have to check with Byron about the repairs, but it should be any time, now."

"What are you doing about security?"

"Byron's takin' care of that, too."

"You put a lot of faith in Byron, don't you?" Clint asked.

"He's my first mate. I have to rely on him."

"Well," Clint said, "I'd like to meet your other crew members, including those who work in your gambling salon."

"Let's go up on deck and see who we can find," Henry said. "Unless you want to have a look at your cabin."

"No," Clint said, "but I do want to see where you've put my horse."

"Then let's go do that first."

***

Henry took Clint below deck, to where the stock was kept. They found Eclipse off in his own corner, away from the pigs and mules.

"Mules?" Clint asked.

"We sometimes need to haul heavy freight."

"I didn't know you transported freight," Clint said, then, looking at the pigs, "or livestock."

"Lately I've been doin' whatever I have to do, Clint,

to keep my boat."

Clint took the time to examine Eclipse. He was in fine fettle, had been fed and brushed, and was comfortably accommodated.

"Well?"

"He looks good," Clint said. "Let's just keep him away from the other livestock, though."

"You've got it."

***

They went back up top and Henry started introducing Clint to crew members. Some shook hands with him, seemingly impressed, while others acted as if they couldn't understand what he was doing there.

Later, they went to the gambling salon so he could meet his "colleagues."

"What have you got here besides poker?" Clint asked.

"We've got a roulette wheel, a Faro dealer, and a dice table."

"Sounds pretty full."

"Oh sure," Henry said, "now all we need are some gamblers."

Henry took Clint around to the tables, which were closed at that moment, and allowed him to meet each dealer. The last one they reached was the poker table.

"Clint Adams, meet Ed Lockhart."

The dealer, who had been playing a hand of solitaire, paused and looked up.

"Adams," he said.

"Hello, Ed."

"You two know each other?" Henry asked, showing surprise.

"We've met a time or two," Clint said.

"Across the table."

"Oh, you've played against each other?" Henry asked.

"We've played at the same table," Clint said. "With other players. It's not the same as playing against each other."

"Cap'n?"

Henry turned to speak to a crewman, then said to Clint, "I'll be right back."

He left the salon

Clint sat down across from Ed Lockhart, who had gathered the cards and was dealing another hand of solitaire.

"I hope this isn't going to be a problem, Ed," Clint said. "Henry didn't tell me you were the dealer on the boat."

"That figures," Lockhart said.

"What do you mean?"

"How well do you know Captain Henry?" Lockhart asked, placing a red Jack on a black Queen.

"We've been friends for some years. I was there when he first got the Natchez Queen."

"But have you seen him lately?"

"No, not lately."

"Well, take my advice," Lockhart said, "and be careful what you agree to. He'll do anything and say anything to get his way."

Clint stared at the man as he set a black three on a red four, and wondered if he was speaking from simple experience, or resentment that Henry had brought Clint on board.

FOURTEEN

Henry returned and took Clint away from Ed Lockhart's poker table.

Outside on deck Henry asked, "What's the story with you and Ed?"

"Oh, it's not important."

"No, come on, now," Henry said, "if there's going to be trouble I'd like to know why."

"How long has he been dealing for you?"

"A couple of years."

"How did he get the job?"

"I needed a dealer, he applied for the job, I gave it to him,. Why, is he not a good poker player."

"He's good enough, I suppose. The fact is...he's a terrible loser."

"So you beat him when you played?"

"To tell you the truth," Clint sais, "everybody beat him."

"So I should get rid of him?"

"I didn't say that," Clint said. "He's not playing any Bat Mastersons or Luke Shorts, here."

"He's not playin' anyone here," Henry said. "All he does is deal."

"So he's just a house dealer, and you take a percentage of every pot?"

"Right."

"Well," Clint said, "He's perfectly qualified for that job."

"That's good to hear," Henry said. "Is there anythin' else you want to do?"

"I think it's time to take a look at my cabin," Clint said, "but first I'd like to meet that cook of yours and congratulate him on his beer."

"He'd be in the galley now," Henry said. "Come this way..."

***

After meeting the cook and talking to him about the beer, Henry showed Clint to his cabin.

"We should be shovin' off any time now," Henry said. "Don't panic when you feel the boat movin'."

"I'll try not to. When do you want me to start playing?"

"You can come to the salon tonight and we'll set up your table. There are a few passengers on board now who will want to play. Then at our next stop, hopefully we'll have more."

"You expect to pick up more passengers based on my name that quickly?"

"Well," Henry said, "I must admit, I have been passin' the word for some time now."

"What?" Clint asked. "Without knowing whether of not I'd agree?"

Henry slapped Clint on the back. "I had a feelin' you wouldn't let me down."

Clint watched Henry walk away, wondering if Ed Lockhart had been speaking from experience, after all.

***

As Clint entered the cabin, Charlotte turned to face him.

"That poor girl!" she cried.

"What's wrong?" Clint asked, seeing the tears in her eyes.

"She's pregnant with her first child, living on this boat, and married to a man who's in love with his boat."

"You don't think she wants to be here?"

"She wants to be where he is," Charlotte said, "but his main concern should be paying attention to her, and their baby."

"He's trying to keep their boat going sothey'll be able to support their baby."

"Men!" she said, walking to the door.

"Where are you going?" he asked.

"To my own cabin!"

She slammed the door behind her.

FIFTEEN

Just moments later, when Clint felt the boat begin to move, he went up on deck. He watched the docks as they pulled away, eyes sharp for anyone paying special attention to them.

He knew Henry Morgan was the Captain, but not the pilot. Still, he'd be up on the bridge as they shoved off. On the other hand, the first mate, Byron Stanhope, was also on deck, eyeing the docks as they pulled away. Clint walked over to stand next to him.

"Anything?" he asked.

"Excuse me?" Stanhope spoke without taking his eyes from the docks.

"I didn't see anyone paying special attention to the Natchez Queen as we pulled away, did you?" Clint asked.

Now Stanhope looked at Clint, considered his words for a moment, then said, "No, I didn't."

"Are you thinking your saboteur was already on board when you left New Orleans?"

"That is what I'm thinking, yes," the first mate said. "Did Cap'n Morgan ask you to help me with security?"

"No," Clint said, "he told me you were in charge. I'm just here to help, if you need it."

"I appreciate that, sir," Stanhope said. "I will let you know."

Clint nodded, turned and walked away. He wasn't at

THE GUNSMITH #417 - ACE HIGH

all sure that the first mate was the man for the job, but that was only because he didn't know him. And because there had already been a good amount of sabotage to the boat. But Henry had told him that the ‚mate was in charge of security, and had only asked Clint to do one thing—play poker.

"Hey Clint!"

He turned, saw Henry coming towards him.

"Would you like to come up to the bridge, take a look at the wheelhouse?"

"Sure thing, Henry. Let's go."

He followed Morgan up to the bridge, where the captain opened the door to the wheelhouse and let him precede him. There was a small, slender man there, standing at the wheel. He looked about forty-five, or so.

"This is our pilot, Andy Abellard."

"Hey, where ya at?" the man said. Clearly, he was a native of New Orleans.

"How are you?" Clint replied.

"I saw you talking with the first mate as we pulled away from the dock," Morgan said to him.

"Just offering him my help," Clint said.

"What was his response?"

"He pretty much said he'd call me if he needed me."

"He's a proud man," Henry Morgan said. "I know this sabotage is somethin' he's takin' personally."

"Well," Clint said, "I hope he's up to the task."

From the wheelhouse he could see the docks as they got smaller behind them.

"I didn't notice anybody particularly interested in the Natchez Queen from the dock," Clint said.

"I think it only matters who's on board," Henry said. "Nobody on the dock can hurt us."

"Did you take on any new passengers at this stop?"

"No," Henry said, "and no one disembarked. All the same people are still aboard."

"That's good. Tonight I can get to meet some of them."

"Yes, you will," Henry said. "At your table."

"And, I thought, in the dining room."

"Will you be eating with us?" Henry asked.

"Why wouldn't I?"

"I thought you might want to eat in your cabin with your guest."

"Charlotte seems to be mad at men, at the moment."

"All men?"

"That's how it seems."

"What happened?"

Clint didn't want to tell Henry that it was after a conversation with his wife.

"I have no idea," he said. "You know how women can get."

"Well, I know how Louisa gets," Henry said, "but she has an excuse. She's pregnant."

"I can't give Charlotte any excuses," Clint said. "If she wants to eat with me, it'll have to be in the dining room."

"I'm sure there are several ladies on board who might be interested in takin' her place." He winked.

"I don't think I need to go looking for that kind of trouble, right now," Clint said. "Not in this confined space."

"I don't blame you for that," Henry said. "Shall we go back down? I need to check on the last of the repairs."

"I'm ready."

The pilot, intent on what was happening in front of him, waved to them both without turning his head or averting his eyes from the river.

Back on deck Henry said, "I'll see you at supper, then, in the dining room. You can sit at my table—with Charlotte, if she likes."

"I'll see if she's still talking to me," Clint said.

SIXTEEN

"I'm sorry," Charlotte said, when she let him into her cabin. "I was upset after talking to Louisa, mad at her husband, and I took it out on you."

"I understand," he said, stepping inside.

"And what also makes me mad is that she's not mad," Charlotte went on.

"She loves her husband."

"I know that," she said, "but even if I had a husband and loved him, he'd have to show me that he loves me, as well. I would not blindly follow him."

"You're a very modern woman," Clint observed.

"Yes, I am," she said. "It gets me into trouble, sometimes, but there it is. I can't change who I am."

"And I wouldn't want you to."

"Why are you here?" she asked. "I know we're moving, but—"

"The captain has invited us to dine with him at his table tonight," Clint said. "He and his wife, that is."

"I'd be happy to dine with Louisa," she said. "If her husband is there, I'll just have to put up with it."

"Okay," Clint said, "let's just be careful what we say in front of Henry."

"Why is that?"

"Because," Clint said, "he could always make us walk the plank."

THE GUNSMITH #417 - ACE HIGH

"The plank?" she asked. "You're kidding, right?"

"About the plank, yes," he said.

"All right, then, I'll be on my best behavior. Okay?"

"Okay," he said. "Thanks."

"And thank you."

"For what?"

"For having them prepare my own cabin."

"I didn't want to assume anything," Clint said. "Besides, I'm sure we'll both be needing some time alone."

"Yes," she said, "we will."

"So I'll get myself ready for supper. Come back for me in an hour."

He nodded, then left the cabin.

***

Carl Tobin waited in the hold of the ship, where the livestock was being kept. It smelled, specifically of the pigs, but this was the only place he and his partner, Bill Grant, could meet without being seen.

"Hey," Grant said, finally appearing.

"What the fuck—" Tobin said. "I've been waitin' here forever and it stinks like hell."

"Sorry," Grant said. "I couldn't get away from the first mate."

"Look," Tobin said, "we gotta do somethin' big. They already fixed everythin' else we did."

"Big?" Grant said. "How big?"

"Really big."

"Like...sink the boat?"

"No," Tobin said, "not that big. Jesus, we're supposed to make him lose the boat because he can't pay his bills, not actually leave it at the bottom of the Mississippi."

"What about St. Louis?" Grant asked. "We can really do somethin' big in St. Louis."

"Yeah, yeah," Tobin said, "we just have to figure out what."

"And when we get there we can send a telegram to the boss," Grant went on.

"And tell him what?" Tobin demanded. "That we ain't done the job yet? No, no telegrams."

"You ain't in charge here, Tobin."

"Well, I better be," Tobin said, "because you ain't gettin' the job done."

"Well, either are you."

Tobin glared at Grant, who was smaller and younger than he was. A big, hulking man, he decided to use his size to intimidate his young partner.

Grant, at twenty-nine, ten years younger and more than half a foot smaller than Tobin, shrank back as the other man advanced on him.

"You're gonna do exactly what I tell ya to do, do ya hear me, Grant?"

"Yeah, yeah, okay, Tobin," Grant said. "Whatever ya say. Just...take it easy."

"Next time we agree to meet here, you're gonna get here first."

"S-sure, sure."

"And no telegram to the boss until I say so."

"R-right, right," Grant said.

"Now get back to work in the galley," Tobin said. "You'll be hearin' from me."

"Yeah, yeah..." Grant got out of there fast, leaving Tobin alone with the pig smell.

SEVENTEEN

When the door opened Clint was stunned.
"What's wrong?" Charlotte asked.
"You look...amazing."

She smiled. "Thank you. I thought this would be the place to wear a dress like this."

"A dress like this" was a lavender gown that showed off her bare, creamy skinned shoulders and upper breasts. Men weren't going to be able to keep their eyes off of her.

"Is it too much?" she asked, suddenly, because he was still staring.

"No, not at all," he said. "A gambling riverboat *is* just the place for it." He extended his arm to her. "Shall we?"

She entwined her arm with his and said, "Thank you."

Closing the door behind they made their way to the upper deck.

***

When they entered the dining room it was only about half full. Mostly men, but there were some women, and they all stopped to watch the couple walk across the floor to the captain's table.

"Charlotte!" Louisa exclaimed, standing up. "You look stunning!"

The two women embraced while Clint and Henry shook hands.

"Wow!" Henry said.

"I know," Clint said.

They all sat.

"Just the four of us?" Clint asked.

"That's it," Henry said. "I don't particularly want to eat with any of these other people."

Louisa and Charlotte were talking already, their heads close together, so Clint figured he was going to have to converse with Henry all through dinner.

Clint looked around the room, didn't see any of the other crew members, or gambling staff from the salon.

"What about the others?" he asked. "They don't eat here?"

"The others?"

"You know, Like Ed, or some of the other dealers—"

"Crew doesn't eat in here," Henry said. "Only guests."

"I'm eating in here," Clint said.

"But you're here with Charlotte, who's a guest."

"What are Ed and the others going to think when they see me in here?"

"They won't see you, because they don't come in here."

"But I won't be eating where they eat," Clint said. "They'll notice that."

"Are you telling me you don't want to eat in here?" Henry asked. "You've had Terry's beer, but wait until you taste his cookin'."

"Doesn't he cook for the crew?"

"Not the way he cooks for the guests."

Clint wondered how the crew felt about the way their Captain treated them? And if some of them didn't like it, would they take it out on him by sabotaging his boat?

"Here comes Terry," Henry said. "Just tell him what you want and he'll make it for you."

"Okay," Clint said.

The ladies both ordered roast chicken, while Clint and Henry asked for steaks.

"With all the trimmings, Terry," Henry said. "Don't forget that."

"I won't, boss," Terry said. "Uh, and to drink?"

Henry lowered his voice.

"No beer in the dining room yet, Terry," Morgan said. "We'll have wine."

"Comin' up, boss."

Terry took one last look at Charlotte's cleavage before leaving the table.

A waiter came back with two bottles of wine—one red, one white—and poured their glasses full.

"I'd like to make a toast," Morgan said, holding his glass high, to my beautiful wife, and our baby."

"To Louisa..." Clint said.

". . . and the baby," Charlotte said.

Clint looked at Charlotte and raised his eyebrows. He hoped she was happy with the toast coming from the loving husband and proud poppa.

Two waiters bought their dinners and soon the table was covered with delicious food.

Charlotte leaned over to her left so she could speak to Clint.

"Did you tell him to do that?"

"Not at all," Clint said. "That was all his idea. He loves his wife, and he's excited about the baby."

"We'll see," she said, "if he's as excited about the

baby as he is about his boat."

"Well," Clint said, "right now I'm excited about my steak. So let's eat."

EIGHTEEN

"After dessert," Morgan said, "you and I will go to the salon and get our table up and going."

"That suits me," Clint said.

They were more than halfway through their meal, and Charlotte and Louisa still had their heads together. Clint hoped Charlotte wasn't telling Louisa what she told Clint about Henry Morgan.

"What did you think of the steak?" Henry asked.

"It was great," Clint said. "The kid's a great cook—great steak, and beer."

"Yes, he's real talented."

"Wait until you taste dessert."

"I'm not a big fancy dessert guy," Clint said. "Pie is usually good enough for me."

"Pie?"

"Yes," Clint said, "peach pie."

"Um, I don't know if we have any—"

"Or whatever kind of pie he has."

"I'll find out," Henry said. He stood up and walked to the galley.

"Where'd he go off to?" Louisa asked.

"I think I caused a problem about dessert," Clint said.

"He's so proud of Terry," Louisa said.

"It seems as if he's proud of everything that has to do with this boat," Charlotte said.

"What? Oh, I see what you mean," Louisa said.

"Do you?"

"Charlotte—" Clint said, warningly.

"No, Clint," Louisa said, "it's all right. Charlotte and I have talked, very frankly. I know what she thinks of Henry, and I still like her. She's very honest."

"Yes, she is," Clint said.

"But she also knows I love my husband," Louisa said. "Right, Charlotte?"

"Right," Charlotte said.

"And I know what I'm doing."

"Yes," Charlotte said, "you do."

Clint wasn't so sure Charlotte was being sincere, this time. But Louisa, on the other hand, seemed to know exactly what she was doing.

"Oh, here comes Henry," Louisa said.

Clint looked and saw Henry walking back across the dining room.

"And what's he carrying?" Louisa asked. "It looks like—"

"—a piece of pie," Clint finished.

NINETEEN

After supper, and dessert, Henry and Clint left the ladies still drinking coffee at the table while they went to the gambling salon.

"Why the word salon?" Clint asked, as they walked. "Why not hall, or just saloon?"

"'Salon' has more class, don't you think?"

"Yeah, and maybe that fits in New Orleans, but here, on the river?"

"Granted, it wouldn't fit in Abilene or Tombstone," Henry said, "but here on the river I think it's perfect."

"Well," Clint said, with a shrug, "it's your boat."

"Yes, it is."

They entered the saloon and Henry led Clint to a table that was covered with a cloth. When he removed it, Clint expected something decorative and spectacular, but it was simply a wooden table—with the top waxed to a high shine, but still just a table.

"Sorry," Henry said, "I couldn't get any green felt in time."

"That's okay," Clint said. "It's just a table."

"And there seem to be a few people who would like

to sit at it," Henry said, looking around.

"I just need some cards, some chips," Clint said.

"On the way."

Clint looked across the room, saw a man walking toward them carrying those things. He also saw Ed Lockhart, already busy with a full table. But, even as he watched, he saw two players cash out and stand up.

"This isn't going to be good," he said to Henry, "if players leave Ed's table to come to mine."

"Relax," Henry said, as the man reached them with the chips and cards, "I had a talk with Ed and he understands."

"Does he?"

"He does," Henry said. "He's a professional."

Clint sat at his table, which was situated so that he sat with his back to a wall. He opened the fresh deck of cards and began to shuffle them, set the caddy of chips next to his left elbow.

The two players reached his table and one of them said, "Mind if we sit down?"

"That's what I'm here for," Clint said.

The two men sat.

"Well," Henry said, "I'll leave you to it. This is Emmett." He pointed to the man who had brought the cards and chips. "If you need anything, like a drink, just ask him."

"Right."

"My name's James," the first man said.

"Samuel," the second man said. "You can call me Sam, Mr. Adams."

"If we're playing poker," Clint said, "you'll have to call me Clint."

"This is amazing," James said, "playing poker with the Gunsmith." He was in his 30's, clearly very impressed.

"You've played with all the best," Samuel said. He was in his 40's, also impressed but trying to cover it up.

"I've lost to all the best," Clint said. "How about we play some draw for a while?"

"That's fine with me," James said.

"You're the boss...Clint," Samuel said. "Deal."

"Let's play a one dollar ante, for now. Later we can lower it, or make it higher. But first you'll have to buy chips."

Both men exchanged cash for chips, and then they all tossed a one dollar chip into the pot.

"Coming out," Clint said, and started to deal.

***

Two hours later he was dealing to four men, and the house was
well ahead. Across the floor, Ed Lockhart was once again dealing himself some hands of Solitaire. Clint knew he was going to take the blame for that.

He knew Lockhart longer than Henry Morgan did, but Morgan's acquaintance was more recent. Maybe Lockhart had changed. Maybe he did understand. But then Clint remembered the things he'd told him about Henry, and maybe he hadn't changed, so much.

He could hear the ball at the roulette wheel as it bounced around on the spinning wheel. He also could hear comments and chips at the blackjack and faro tables. There weren't many players in the room, though, but he had the most seated at his table. Maybe Henry was right, maybe they'd pick up some more in St. Louis, or wherever their next stop would be.

***

THE GUNSMITH #417 - ACE HIGH

After a couple of more hours, Ed Lockhart apparently got tired of playing solitaire—and drinking—and wandered over to Clint's table to watch. He brought a large glass of red wine with him.

"You fellas were havin' more luck ay my table," he said to James and Sam.

"That may be," James said, "but at least we're losin' to the Gunsmith"

"And we're learnin' somethin' over here," Samuel said.

"And you weren't learnin' nothin' at my table?" Lockhart slurred.

Clint had not raised his hand to Emmett the entire night, but now he did, indicating to the man that he wanted him to come over.

Emmett came up alongside him and said, "Sir?" He was a large man with an impressive set of muttonchops that made it difficult to guess his age.

"Get him away from my table, Emmett," Clint said.

"Yes, sir."

"Do it gently," Clint added. "He's been drinking. Maybe get him to his cabin, and close his table."

"Yes, sir."

Emmett sidled up alongside Lockhart, who was still talking to James and Sam, trying to convince them to come back to his table. The big man said something to him that only Lockhart could hear.

"What the hell are you talkin' about?" Lockhart demanded. "I'm perfectly fine!"

Emmett spoke softly to him again.

"Goddamn it, Emmett. Get away from me-now!" He was cut off when Emmett wrapped one large hand around his upper arm. He squeezed, causing Lockhart to lose the strength in that hand. He would have dropped his wine glass to the floor, but Emmett grabbed it with his other hand.

"Let's go, sir!" Emmett said, and walked Lockhart away from the table and off the gambling floor, out of the salon completely. Despite the man's continued protests.

"Well," James said, "glad he's gone. Now it's quiet, again."

"He's certainly not the poker player you are, Clint," Sam said.

"He's had his moments," Clint said.

"Have you played with him?" James asked.

"A time or two."

"So he's played against the same people you have?" Sam asked.

"Some of them."

"He must have lost a lot of money," James observed.

"Over the years," Clint said, "we're all lost a lot of money."

"But what about—" James started. Clint cut him off.

"Do you gents want to talk, or play?"

"Let's play," one of the other gamblers said. "I'm tired of all the talkiin'."

"Coming out, then," Clint said. "Let's play some seven card stud."

***

As the hour got later and later the men quit one by one, until once again it was Clint, James and Sam. Clint started to deal five card stud. The other tables in the salon had closed. The bar was still open, but there was only the bartender and Emmett standing at it. Emmett made a signal to Clint, which he took to mean it was time to close up.

"Last card, gents," Clint said. "Table's closed after this."

"Already?" James asked.

"It's after two a.m.," Clint said.

"Didn't realize it was that late," Sam said.

Clint dealt the last cards, they made their bets and showed their hoe card. Sam won the hand, which made him happy.

"At least I win the last hand of the night," he said, raking in his chips.

TWENTY

Clint slept alone in his cabin. He did not knock on Charlotte's door, and she did not knock on his. He had the feeling she was still unhappy with men, in general.

In the morning he rose, washed, and left the cabin. He was hungry, wondering where he should go for breakfast. Before reaching deck, he ran into Henry Morgan.

"Ah, on your way to breakfast," Henry said. "So am I. Let's walk."

As they made their way to the deck, Henry asked. "How did the first night go?"

"I won," Clint said. "Do I turn the profits over to you?"

"No, no," Henry said, "those are yours."

"I keep the profits, and you're paying me?"

"You also will suffer your own losses," Henry said.

"Ah."

When they reached the doors to the dining room, Clint suddenly stopped.

"Where does the crew and staff eat?" Clint asked.

"Don't start that, again," Henry said. "They all know that we're friends. They don't expect you to eat with them. You're not just another member of the staff."

Clint was still thinking when the fragrance of breakfast came to him from the space between the double

THE GUNSMITH #417 - ACE HIGH

doors.

"Oh, all right," he said, and they entered.

Once again Clint dined at the captain's table with Henry Morgan, only this time without Charlotte and Louisa.

"Where's Charlotte this mornin'?" Morgan asked.

"I don't know," Clint said.

"Didn't see her last night?"

"Not after supper," Clint said. "After I closed my table, I returned to my cabin and went to sleep. What about Louisa?"

"She decided to have breakfast in our cabin, this mornin'."

"Was she upset?"

Henry frowned. "About what?'

"Uh, I just thought, maybe something that was said at the table last night?"

"No," Henry said, "not that I know of. She does the paperwork for the boat, and she decided to eat breakfast while she worked."

"I see."

A waiter came and took their breakfast order, then brought them coffee.

"So, no problems last night?"

Clint hesitated. He didn't know whether or not Emmett had talked to Henry, already.

"Ed got kind of drunk," Clint said. "I had to have Emmett walk him away from my table."

"Oh," Henry said, frowning. "As long as he's worked here, I've never seen him drunk."

"Well, players from his table got up and came to mine," Clint said. "Soon he was playing solitaire, then he started drinking. Eventually, he came walking over to my table and started in on them."

"Jesus."

"I signaled to Emmett and asked him to remove Lockhart, take him to his cabin. Hopefully, he slept it off. And hopefully, it won't happen again."

"I'll talk to him."

"You should," Clint said.

"I will," Henry said. "You know, I could fire him, if you'd agree to stay—"

"I'm here temporarily," Clint said, cutting him off. "Don't fire him."

"All right."

The waiter brought their plates and they began to eat. Little by little the passengers began to come in. Clint saw the two men who had left Lockhart's table. They were eating separately, and alone. He also saw the other two men who had joined the game later. They were eating together.

"The men I played with last night are here," Clint said.

"Where?"

"There, there, and there," Clint said, pointing. "Do you know anything about them?"

"James Adair," Henry said. "This is his second trip upriver with us. All he does is play poker. He probably got tired of playing with Lockhart."

"And the other?"

"Samuel Folds," Henry said. "His first time with us. He's some kind of businessman."

"And those two?"

Henry frowned. "It's their first time with us, too. I don't know their names, off hand."

"Did they arrive together?"

"Uh, no, I don't think so," Henry said. "I think they have separate cabins."

THE GUNSMITH #417 - ACE HIGH

"Have they eaten breakfast together before?"

"I can't say that I've noticed," Henry admitted. "Why?"

"I'm interested in all your passengers," Clint said. "I just happened to meet these four first. While we were playing none of them seemed to particularly know each other. Now those two are eating together."

"Maybe they made friends at your table."

"Not *at* my table," Clint said.

"Then after."

"What about the waiter at their table?" Clint asked.

Henry looked over. It was a different waiter than the one who had served them.

"Maybe he'd know if they've eaten together before."

"We can ask him."

"Not obviously," Clint said.

"Then how?"

"Have our waiter ask their waiter in the galley," Clint said.

"All right," Henry said. "I'll call him over."

"Let's wait til he comes over on his own," Clint said.

They started to eat.

"What's your first mate been doing?" Clint asked.

"His job," Henry said.

"I mean about the sabotage."

"I don't know," Henry said.

"Doesn't he report to you?"

"Not every moment."

"Has he looked into the passengers?"

"I assume so."

"Henry," Clint said, "you have to do more than assume. You have to be more involved."

"He's my First Mate, Clint," Henry said. "I have to depend on him."

"Let me ask you a question, then."

"Go ahead."

"What if Byron is the saboteur?"

Henry stopped with his fork halfway to his mouth.

"Never thought of that."

TWENTY-ONE

When the waiter came back with more coffee, Henry gave him his instructions.

"You want me to do what?" the man asked.

"Arthur, I want you to ask David if the two men at that table," Henry inclined his head but did not point, "have eaten together before this mornin'."

"And that's all?"

"That's it."

Arthur turned and looked at the two men.

"I don't have to, Captain."

"Why not?"

"I've served them before."

"Separately, or together?" Clint asked.

"Separately."

"So they don't always sit in the same place?" Clint asked.

Arthur looked at his Captain.

"Answer his question, Arthur."

The waiter looked at Clint.

"No, sir, they don't," he said, "this is the first time I've seen them sitting together."

"All right, then," Clint said, nodding to Henry.

"It's okay, Arthur," Henry said. "You don't need to talk to David."

"Yes, sir. Anything else, Captain?"

THE GUNSMITH #417 - ACE HIGH

"Not right now."

They waited until Arthur walked away.

"So what does that tell us?" Henry asked Clint.

"That they're probably not the saboteurs. At least not together, anyway."

"Why not?"

"Because if they were," Clint said, "they wouldn't want to be seen together."

"But one of them could still be?"

"Oh, yes," Clint said.

Henry looked over at the two men.

"Which one?"

"That's the question," Clint said. He looked around. "It could be anyone in this room."

At that moment the double doors opened and a woman walked in, immediately catching Clint's attention. She was tall, slender but shapely, with very, very black hair.

"Even her," he said. "Who is that?"

"Ah, that's Miss Adelaide Buckley," Henry said. "She boarded in New Orleans."

"And where is she going?"

"Upriver, was all she said."

They watched as she walked to a table, sat down and was immediately approached by both waiters working the room. All the other men in the room were also watching.

"Why didn't I see her last night?" Clint said. "She didn't eat here, or gamble."

"Well," Henry said, "as far as I know, she doesn't gamble. And I guess she ate in her cabin, last night."

"So she usually eats in here in the evenings?" Clint asked.

"As far as I know, yes," Henry said. "She's hard to

ignore, and I've noticed her in here most evenings."

"Is she traveling with anyone?"

"No," Henry said, "she's alone."

"Uh-huh."

"But you're not," Henry said.

"What?"

"Need I remind you about Charlotte?"

"I only met Charlotte a day or two ago," Clint said. "Besides, she's not very happy with men, right now."

"Why's that?"

Clint studied Henry for a moment, then said, "Well, apparently, she's not happy with the way you've been treating your pregnant wife."

"What?" Henry said. "What's wrong with the way I treat Louisa?"

"You're making her live on this boat while she's pregnant," Clint said. "Charlotte doesn't think this is the place for a pregnant wife to live."

"Has she talked to Louisa about this?"

"Well," Clint said, "they have their heads together quite a lot, don't they?"

"Yeah, they do," he said. "I guess they've become friends very quickly."

"And friends talk," Clint said, "especially women."

Henry frowned.

"Do you think I mistreat my wife?"

"Hey," Clint said, "that's between you and your wife." He was still looking across the room at Miss Adelaide Buckley.

"Maybe I should ask her if she'd rather live somewhere else," Henry said.

"And what would you do if she said yes?" Clint asked. "I mean, about the boat?"

"I...don't know," Henry said. "Stop tryin' to save it?"

"And do what?" Clint asked. "You're a riverboat Captain, right?"

"Right."

"And she knows that."

"Right, again."

"So if she doesn't want to live on the boat, you'd have to put her somewhere else, like...New Orleans? Then you'd have to spend a lot of time apart."

"You have a point," Henry said. "We like spendin' time together."

"And she does your paperwork."

"And you're right, still again."

"So never mind what Charlotte thinks," Clint said. "It only matters what the two of you think."

"And what are you thinkin', right now?" Henry asked, picking up his coffee cup.

"I'm thinking that," Clint said, inclining his head toward Miss Adelaide Buckley, "is a beautiful woman."

TWENTY-TWO

There was no gambling during the day, so there was no rush to finish breakfast. Adelaide Buckley was eating in a very leisurely fashion.

"How did you meet Charlotte?" Henry asked.

"In a café, while we were both eating."

"Like now?"

"Kind of like now," Clint said, "except that she called me over to her table."

"Well," Henry said, "it doesn't look like that's going to happen here."

"Probably not." Clint reluctantly took his eyes from the woman and looked at his friend. "What kind of shape is your boat in?"

"All repairs have been made," Henry said. "We're in tip-top shape right now. At least, until the saboteur strikes again."

"Maybe they'll be found before that," Clint said.

"They?" Henry said. "You think there's more than one?"

"Could be," Clint said. "What does Byron think? Oh, wait, you don't ask him those kinds of questions."

"Now, look—"

"I know," Clint said, "you depend on him."

"I do," Henry said, "but while you're here it would be silly of me not to take advantage of your, uh, experience."

"You mean, other than my poker playing?"

"Well," Henry said, "if you think there might be more than one, then maybe Byron could use a little help."

"He doesn't think so."

"I'll talk to him," Henry said.

"Just ask him some questions, Henry," Clint said. "Find out where he is in his investigation."

"And I'll tell him to let you help him."

"No," Clint said, "just suggest to him that he might put me to use while I'm here. Don't *tell* him."

"Well, I'm the captain, he'd have to—oh, all right," Captain Henry Morgan said. "I'll just make a suggestion."

"Good." Clint stood up. "I'm going to take a walk around deck, have a look at the whole boat."

"Just do me a favor."

"What's that?"

"Don't fall uverboard," Henry said. "They don't call it the muddy Mississippi for nothin'. We might not be able to find you."

"I'll keep that in mind."

On the way to the salon doors, Clint walked past Adelaide Buckley's table. She looked up and their eyes met briefly. He nodded and smiled, and she returned it, then went back to her meal.

Yeah, he had enough trouble without looking for more.

***

He walked around the entire boat, taking everything in, even looking over the side at the muddy Mississippi. In the rear of the boat he spent some time watching the paddlewheel go around. He hadn't asked Henry Morgan the specifics about the sabotage, but what better way to damage a riverboat like this than to destroy the paddlewheel in some way.

He exchanged nods and glances with passengers and crew alike, as he worked his way back up the other side of the boat. He didn't know port from starboard, stem from stern, even though Sam Clemens had tried to teach him at one time. All he knew was that the boat had a front and back, and two sides, and he walked it all, keeping a wary eye out for trouble.

At this portion of the river, neither side of the shore seemed very far away, but he knew the Mississippi widened and narrowed, sometimes in the blink of an eye. Even bends in the river were known to straighten themselves out. That was why an experienced man was needed at the wheel.

As he reached the front of the boat, he saw the first mate, Byron Stanhop, talking to a few of the crewmen. He doubted that Henry had had time to talk with the man yet, so he did as he had done with all the others he'd past, and simply nodded. Instead of a return nod, he got a glare.

Helping this man in his search for the saboteur was not going to be easy.

TWENTY-THREE

When he returned to his cabin the strong smell of perfume right outside the door told him he had either had a visitor, or still did. He went inside.

"There you are," Charlotte said. "I was looking for you."

"Sorry," Clint said. "I had breakfast with the captain, and then took a long walk around the boat to see what's what."

"I thought you said you've seen this boat before?"

"Years ago," he said. "Sorry I didn't knock on your door for breakfast."

"That's okay," she said. "I had breakfast with Louisa in her cabin."

"Oh, really?" he asked, closing the door. Charlotte was seated in a chair at the table in the room, wearing a simple blue dress that covered her skin, but did not hide her shape. "And what did you talk about?"

"Apparently," Charlotte said, "she's heard everything I've had to say, but would like me to stop criticizing her husband."

"You didn't have a fight, did you?"

"Not at all," Charlotte said. "We've become fast friends. I just have to watch what I say if I want us to stay that way."

"And what do you intend to do?"

"Well," she said, "I'm not going to say bad things about Morgan the Pirate to his wife," she said. "Just to you."

"He is my friend," Clint said. "I don't think I'd like to hear any more negative remarks about him."

She stood up.

"So you don't want to hear from me anymore?"

"I didn't say that."

"Clint," she said, "I have to voice my opinions."

"Why can't you just think them?" he asked. "And keep it to yourself."

"In other words," she said, "shut up!"

"I didn't say that, eith—"

"Never mind," she said, walking to the door. "I get the message."

"Charlotte—" he said, but she was out the door, slamming it behind her.

He wondered what the rest of the ride upriver was going to be like?

***

Clint had finished reading THE PRINCE AND PAUPER, and had moved on to Alexander Dumas THE THREE MUSKETEERS. He spent the afternoon in his cabin, reading, until it was time to get dressed to go back to the dining room for dinner. He knew that he'd be at the Captain's table with Henry and Louisa, he just wasn't sure if Charlotte would be there.

Before leaving Natchez on the Queen, Clint had brought two suits that would make him look like a proper gambler. He hadn't worn one the night before, but he changed into one now and looked in the mirror. He reminded himself of the late Doc Holliday.

He left the cabin and headed for the dining room.

***

As he'd expect, Charlotte was not at the table with Henry and Louisa.

"Where's Charlotte?" Louisa asked, as he sat with them.

"I think she's angry with me," Clint said.

"Oh, no!" Louisa said, putting her hands to her face. "Maybe it was me."

"No, not you," Clint said.

"What did you do?" Henry asked his wife.

She looked at him. "I asked her to stop saying negative things about you."

"Ah," Henry said. "And what did you do to her?" he asked Clint.

"Same thing, I guess," Clint said. "I told her we were friends and I didn't want to hear anything negative. I told her to keep the thoughts to herself."

"And what was her reaction to that?" Louisa asked.

"She felt like I was telling her to shut up."

"That can't be good," Henry said.

"That's not something any woman wants to hear," Louisa said, "or even think she's hearing."

"Well," Clint said, "she may put in an appearance, yet."

The waiter came over and they all ordered.

"You're lookin' good in that suit," Henry said.

"Yes," Louisa said, "very handsome."

"Thank you. I thought if I was going to be playing poker night after night, I might as well look the part."

THE GUNSMITH #417 - ACE HIGH

"Well, you do," Louisa said.

"You look just like a gambler," Henry said. "A true riverboat gambler, like George Devol." Devol was famous in the river, as a gambler. "Or Bat Masterson."

"I can't wear a suit the way Bat does," Clint said. "Or gamble the way he does. He's the one you should have here."

"I don't know Bat Masterson," Henry said, "but I do know you. And I'm happy that you're here."

"I just hope that my presence helps you."

The waiter brought their meals, and they continued to talk while they ate.

"Henry told me you walked the entire boat," Louisa said. "What do you think?"

"It's bigger than I remembered," Clint said.

"It may not seem so big if we can get more people on it," Henry said.

"Where's our next stop?" Clint asked.

"We'll be stopping in Vicksburg, Greenville, and Cape Girardeau before we reach St. Louis. We might pick up some more passengers in the smaller towns, but I'm really hoping to pick up a larger number in St. Louis."

"So Vicksburg is next?"

"Yes," Henry said, "tomorrow."

"Well, if you started passing the word when you said you did," Clint said, "I might have more players tomorrow night."

"Let's hope," Henry said.

They both looked at Louisa, saw that she was staring toward the door. When Clint looked that way he thought he might see Charlotte, but instead he saw Adelaide Berkley entering the dining room. She was shown to a table where she sat, alone.

"There's something wrong with that woman," Louisa

said.

"How do you mean?" Clint asked.

Louisa looked at him.

"She sits alone at every meal. I've never seen her speaking to another person on board, other than a waiter."

"Have you ever tried to speak to her?" Clint asked.

"No," Louisa said, "not yet."

"Maybe she's just a private person," Henry said. "Maybe she just wants to be left alone, and that's why she booked passage. I say if that's what she wants, that's what she should have."

"Do you know what she orders?" Clint asked Louisa. "For breakfast, for supper?"

"No," Louisa said, "but she sits at the same table every time, so she has the same waiter."

"And he'd know," Clint finished.

"Why don't we just leave the woman alone?" Henry asked.

Clint looked at him.

"Oh," the Captain said, "you think she might be involved with the sabotage."

"I think everybody on the boat is a suspect," Clint said, "and she has an odd pattern of behavior."

"Wow," Henry said, "you sound like a detective."

"One of my best friends in a private detective," Clint replied, speaking of Talbot Roper. "I've learned quite a few things from him."

TWENTY-FOUR

Clint spent the night playing poker.

James and Samuel sat at his table once again. They came separately, an hour apart. The other two men he'd been playing with did not appear at his table, or in the salon, at all.

Ed Lockhart had two players at his table, which was silly, because essentially, with Lockhart just dealing, the two men were playing head-to-head. For the most part, a head-to-head contest, over the course of many hours, would come out even. Apparently, these two men just wanted to play poker on a Mississippi riverboat.

In Clint's case, he was playing against James and Samuel, so the game was clearly three-handed.

Later in the evening, Clint was surprised when a fourth player appeared at his table.

"May I sit?" Adelaide Buckley asked.

She was wearing a lavender dress, which covered her from shoulders to floor, except for a cut-out section that revealed the swell of her breasts.

James and Sam looked up at her and their eyes went wide. Clint assumed it was only because of who she was and how she looked—or perhaps they were surprised that a woman wanted to play.

"Of course you can sit," Clint said.

She sat down and bought some chips from Clint.

THE GUNSMITH #417 - ACE HIGH

"What are we playing?" she asked.

"Right now, five card stud."

"Excellent."

But Clint didn't start to deal. This was an opportunity he didn't want to waste.

"I haven't seen you in here before," he said.

"You've seen me in the dining room," she said.

"I meant in here, gambling."

"I didn't have any reason to want to gamble, before," she told him.

"And you do now?"

"A chance to play poker against the Gunsmith?" she asked. "That's reason enough, I think."

"I'm flattered."

"Can we play?" James asked. "I've been losing money."

"So have I," Sam said.

"Of course," Adelaide said. "That's why we're here, isn't it? To play?"

"Cards coming out," Clint said, and began to deal.

He gave each player one card down, and then one card face up. In turn, the cards went to James, Adelaide, Sam and then him, as Adelaide had seated herself between the two men.

"Ten of Spades, three of hearts, Jack of clubs," Clint said. "And an eight of diamonds for the dealer."

His hole card was an eight of clubs, giving him a pair on his first two cards. A pair of any kind was an impressive beginning in a game of five card stud.

"Jack bets," he said to Sam.

"Five dollars," Sam said.

"I call," Clint said. A five dollar bet from Sam meant the man might have had another Jack in the hole, or at least, a picture card.

"Call," James said.

"I'll call," Adelaide said. Clint figured her for a pair of threes, otherwise why call?

"Cards," Clint said, and dealt each player their third cards.

A seven for James, no apparent help.

A five of hearts for Adelaide.

A king of diamonds for Sam.

Clint dealt himself a useless deuce of clubs.

"You're still in the lead, this time with a king," he said to Sam. "Your bet."

"Ten dollars," Sam said. His hand hadn't improved, but he was trying to make it seem as if it had.

"I'll call," Clint said.

"Call," James said.

"Sure, why not?" Adelaide said.

Clint dealt the next cards—a six of hearts to James, another three—clubs—to Adelaide, improving her hand; a queen of spades to Sam, and another deuce on his hand, giving him two pair. However, he figured Adelaide for three threes.

But he now had a pair of deuces on the table, which made him second to Adelaide's threes.

"Twenty dollars," she said. It was the biggest bet of the two days.

"Twenty?" Sam frowned, looked at his hole card. Now Clint knew he had a jacks. A pair of jacks would normally be formidable in 5 card stud, but Clint had two pair, and he knew Adelaide had three of a kind. Still, Sam could not bring himself to fold hid jacks. Not with another card coming.

"I call," he said, pushing twenty dollars worth of chips into the swelling pot.

"I call," Clint said. "Twenty to you, James."

THE GUNSMITH #417 - ACE HIGH

"I fold."

"Last card," Clint said.

Nobody's hand improved on the table. Clint knew he was beat by Adelaide. Sam was still frowning at his jacks.

"Twenty dollars," Adelaide said.

Sam completely read the situation wrong. He'd been worried about Clint, who checked. He didn't think that a woman—any woman—was a threat at a poker table, so he now liked his jacks as the winning hand.

"I call," he said. He didn't want to fold, but was not bold enough to raise.

Clint thought he was bit, but wanted to try one raise to see what Adelaide would do.

"Your twenty," he said, "and another."

James—out of the hand—whistled.

"You must like your hand," Adelaide said.

Clint said nothing.

"Oh, all right," she said. "I should raise, but I'll just call."

Sam looked flummoxed. Why had Clint bet? Why did Adelaide think she should raise? There were a pair of threes and a pair of twos on the table.

"I'll raise twenty," he said, his voice tremulous, exposing his nervousness.

"Attaboy, Sam," James said. "Go get 'em."

Sam smiled wanly at the support.

"Sam," Clint said, "you're coming in third this hand, but I'll just call you."

"Yes," Adelaide said, "no point in twisting the knife. I'll call."

Sam hesitated, then turned over his hole card. It was a king, not a jack, but with a pair of kings he was still third.

"Two pair," Clint said, turning over his eight to reveal his eights and threes.

"Three threes," Adelaide said.

"What?" Sam said, staring at her cards.

"I'm sorry, gents," Adelaide said, raking in the chips. "Guess I just got lucky my first hand of the night."

"I guess so," Clint said. "James, it's your deal."

James collected the cards, shuffled and said, "Let's try a hand of draw."

"Suits me" Adelaide said, tossing a chip into the center of the table for her ante.

She smiled at Clint.

TWENTY-FIVE

Adelaide turned out to be a very good poker player. Clint wondered why she had not been playing up until now?

As the hour got later and later, Sam and James each lost their stake and said good-night. Eventually it was just Clint and Adelaide.

"Those two aren't very good players, are they?" she asked.

"I'm afraid not," Clint said. "That's why I've been keeping the stakes low."

"Would you like to raise them, now?"

"Not tonight," Clint said. "It's getting late. But maybe tomorrow night, if you'd care to start playing earlier."

"Maybe I will," she said, "and you're right,. It is getting late, and since the boys left, we're just sending the same chips back and forth. I think I'll cash out."

Clint cashed her out, and then his table was closed.

"How about a drink before you leave?" he asked. "At the bar, on me."

"Sure, why not?"

They got up from the table and walked to the bar. Around them the other tables were also closing, and people were leaving for the night.

At the bar Clint asked, "What would you like?"

"A glass of champagne."

THE GUNSMITH #417 - ACE HIGH

"Champagne for the lady," he said to the bartender, "and a glass of beer for me."

"Comin' up, sir," the bartender said.

When he brought the drinks, Clint picked up the glass of champagne and presented it to Adelaide.

"Thank you."

"You're welcome." He picked up his beer.

She surprised him by drinking the champagne straight down rather than sipping it. Then she put the empty glass down on the bar.

"Thanks for the drink. Good-night."

"Good-night?" he said. "I thought we'd talk a while."

"Well, like you said, it's getting late. We can talk tomorrow night, while we play."

"So you will be playing tomorrow?"

"I'm pretty sure," she said. "I enjoyed tonight. I like winning money from men."

"We might pick up some more players in Vicksburg—"

"That'd be good," she said. "Good-night, Mr. Adams."

"Uh, yeah, good-night...Miss Buckley."

He watched her walk to the doors and out of the salon, wondering what had just happened.

"Pretty lady," the bartender said.

"Yes, she is."

"Doesn't talk much, though, does she?"

Clint looked at the man and said, "No, apparently she doesn't."

"You want another beer before we close up shop for the night?"

"Sure," Clint said, "why not? There's nothing else going on."

112

TWENTY-SIX

"I told you to be here first next time," Carl Tobin told Bill Grant.

"Sorry," Grant said. "I couldn't get away."

"Yeah," Tobin said.

"So what's goin' on?" Grant asked. He looked around in disgust at the pigs.

"We're makin' a move tonight."

"What kind of move?"

"We're gonna poke a hole in the boat," Tobin said.

Grant looked surprised.

"We gonna sink it?"

"No," Tobin said. "We ain't gonna sink it—at least, not with us on it."

"So...we're just gonna poke a hole...someplace?"

"Right around water level."

"And let water in."

"Some."

"But not enough to sink 'er."

"No."

"Okay, how we doin' this?"

"With these." Tobin reached down, came up with two sticks of dynamite.

"Whoa!"

Take it easy," Tobin said.

"You know what you're doin' with that stuff?" Grant

113

asked, nervously.

"Of course I do," Tobin said.

"So when do we do this?"

"In a couple of hours," Tobin said. "It's gettin' late, the gamblin' is shuttin' down, pretty soon everybody will be in their cabins."

"So," Grant asked, "how big a hole will they make?"

"Big enough to hold the boat up for repairs. They won't make Vicksburg, they sure won't make St. Louis."

"What do we do in the meantime?"

"We wait."

"And what do we do after?"

"Our jobs," Tobin said. "Whatever the first mate tells us to do. Remember, we're loyal crew."

"Right, we are."

"Come on," Tobin said, "we'll get into position."

"And wait how long?"

Tobin shrugged. "Coupla hours, maybe."

"Down here?"

"We're gonna get it done, Grant," Tobin said. "Then we can get off this tub."

"It's not a bad boat," Grant said.

"Yeah," Tobin said, "what you see of it from the galley."

TWENTY-SEVEN

Clint left the salon after his second beer. It was dark out, and somewhat foggy. He headed for his cabin, when he thought he heard something. He stopped and listened. Water lapped against the side of the boat. He could hear the paddlewheel churning in the back. How could he have heard anything else?

He stood still and looked around. That's when he thought he saw something—two somethings. Two figures, moving in the darkness. It was only for a moment, and then they were swallowed by the fog.

He could have thought he was imagining it—might have, if not for the fact that there had already been sabotage on the boat. So instead of heading for his cabin, he turned and started walking the other way.

He kept alert, didn't see anything again, but was convinced he wasn't imagining things. He never did. He just didn't have that good of an imagination.

Clint looked around, picked out the spot he thought he saw the two figures in, and went that way. He came to a closed door. He tried it, found it unlocked. Opening it carefully, he listened intently, but couldn't hear anything out of the ordinary. There were stairs leading down, so he decided to follow them.

Once he was inside and the door closed behind him, it was pitch black. He waited a few minutes for his eyes to

THE GUNSMITH #417 - ACE HIGH

adjust. He didn't know how steep the steps were, didn't want to risk falling down them and breaking his neck.

Eventually he was able to make out the stairs in front of him, and began to descend slowly. He could still hear the hum of the paddlewheel turning.

When he reached the bottom, he stopped to listen again. Still the thump-thump-thump of the paddlewheel as the walls seemed to amplify it. He wondered just what part of the boat he was in? He didn't smell livestock.

He began to move again, down a long hallway. He could reach out and touch either wall without stretching his arms.

Then he heard something familiar, and it made his blood run cold. It was a hissing sound he'd heard many times before.

A lit fuse.

He increased his speed and, abruptly, saw the lighted fuse glowing ahead of him, and two men standing over it.

"Hold it!" he said, drawing his gun.

One man froze, while the other ran. When the frozen man finally moved, he turned toward Clint, who didn't know if the man had a gun or not, but he certainly had a stick of dynamite.

Clint fired once, hitting the man in the chest. Then he rushed forward as the man slumped to the floor. The lighted stick of dynamite turned out to be two sticks, tied together. Clint quickly grabbed them up from the floor and pulled the fuse out. Only then did he heave a sigh of relief.

TWENTY-EIGHT

Clint thought about chasing the other man, but decided instead to check the one he'd shot. If he was alive, he could tell Clint who the other man was. Besides, he couldn't very well go running around in the dark.

Clint checked the fallen man. Even in the dark room it was obvious he was dead. He checked his pockets, found some matches and lit one. He examined the man again by the light of the match, careful to keep the flame and the dynamite sticks well apart.

Using more of the matches, he walked in the direction the other man had run, eventually found his way to another set of stairs, which led up to the deck. Looking around, there was no one in sight. He still had the two dynamite sticks in his hand. With little else to do, he went to find both Henry Morgan, and his first Mmate, Byron Stanhope.

***

"This sonofabitch works in the galley," Stanhope said. Both he and Henry were carrying lamps.

"I don't know him," Henry said. "He's not a long time crew member."

"No," Stanhope said, "he signed on in New Orleans, just before we shoved off."

THE GUNSMITH #417 - ACE HIGH

Henry looked at Clint.

"You say there were two men?"

"That's right."

"Would you recognize the other one?"

"No," Clint said, "it was dark, and I was concentrating on the dynamite. Like I said, the fuse was lit."

"Sonsofbitches!" Stanhope swore. "That dynamite would have punched a sizeable hole in this hull."

"How bad would it have been?" Clint asked.

"Pretty bad," the first mate said.

"No, I mean," Clint said, "how far under the water are we? How much water would have come in?"

"Not much," Henry said. "This part of the hull isn't under water. We're just about at water level."

"So it wouldn't have sunk the boat?"

"Not likely," Henry said.

"But we wouldn't be goin' anywhere until we made repairs," Stanhope said.

"So all this sabotage has been carefully planned to damage the boat, but not that much."

"I suppose..." Henry said.

"I'll get some men to haul Grant out of here," Stanhope said. "We'll toss him overboard."

"Not a good idea," Clint said.

"What do you suggest?" Henry asked.

"We hand him over to the law when we get to Vicksburg," Clint suggested, "tell them what happened. They'll want to talk to me, since I killed him."

"Are you gonna get hauled off to jail?" Henry asked. "I mean, with your reputation."

"Probably not," Clint said. "We've got the dynamite to show that he had bad intentions."

"I still say we should toss him overboard," Stanhope said.

"We're gonna do what Clint says!" Henry snapped.

"Can I remind you, Captain, I'm the First Mate, and I'm in charge of the security of this—"

"And who was it who kept these two jaspers from blowin' a hole in my boat?" Henry asked.

The first mate fell silent.

"That's right!" Henry snapped. "I don't know where you were, Byron, or what you were doin', but Clint saved us, and he killed a man doin' it. So we'll play this the way he wants to. You got it?"

"Got it, Cap'n."

"Now you go ahead and get some men to haul this body out of here. And keep this quiet. We don't want the passengers hearin' that there was dynamite on board."

"Aye, Sir."

Stanhope turned and stormed away, his lamp lighting his way.

"Now he really doesn't like me," Clint observed.

"That may be so," Henry Morgan said, "but I'm not too fond of him, at the moment."

TWENTY-NINE

Instead of meeting with Henry in his cabin, they met up on the bridge. Henry didn't want Louisa to hear what had happened. Not yet, anyway.

"I appreciate what you did, Clint," Henry said. "And I'm gonna tell Byron to work with you."

"He won't like it."

"I don't care," Henry said. "You're the one who saved us from a catastrophe."

"You said the boat wouldn't have sunk."

"You never know," Henry said. "That may not have been the intent, but two sticks of dynamite might have done more damage than she could have handled. So as far as I'm concerned, you saved our boat."

"Okay," Clint said, "I'll accept that."

"And we now know we had two saboteurs, and now we have one," Henry went on.

"I wish that was right."

"Why isn't it?"

"Because there could still be others," Clint said. "We don't know how many there were to start with."

"Okay, so then we had at least two," Henry said, "and now we have at least one."

"Yes," Clint said. "Tell me, Henry, how many of your crew members do you absolutely trust?"

"I'm not sure."

"Well, how many have been with you from the beginning?"

"Five or six."

"Including your First Mate?"

"Yes."

"So you trust him."

"Enough to say that he's not one of the saboteurs."

"You're sure of that?"

"Damn, Clint," Henry said, "he loves this boat as much as I do."

"Anybody else love it that much?" Clint asked. "The other five or six crew members?"

"I'd have to think about that."

"Well, think about it overnight and let me know in the morning," Clint said. "At breakfast."

"Okay," Henry said.

"In fact, make me a list," Clint said. "People you know—and I mean *know*—are not involved."

"I'll do that."

"And talk to Louisa about it."

"I was thinkin' I'd keep this from her," Henry said.

"I don't think that's a good idea," Clint said.

"Why not?"

"Well," Clint said, "for one thing, if and when she finds out she'll be furious."

"True."

"And second, she might have something to contribute that you don't."

"Also true," Henry said. "She's a smart girl."

"I'm pretty tired, so I'm going to bed. What did Byron do with that dynamite?"

"That he did throw overboard," Henry said. "He's still mad we didn't let him do that to the body."

"We have to report this to the law in Vicksburg,

Henry."

"You've got to understand, Clint," Henry said, "people on the river have their own law."

"Not this time," Clint said. "I'm not river people, and I only go by one law."

"Okay," Henry said, "whatever you say. I'm just glad you're here—especially tonight."

"You better get some rest, too."

They both left the bridge together and went down to their cabins.

***

Clint smelled perfume outside his door, but it wasn't the same scent Charlotte had been wearing. Maybe she switched. He went inside.

"Well," the girl in the bed said, "I almost fell asleep waiting for you. Luckily, I found a book." She held up the copy of THE THREE MUSKETEERS.

Clint stared at Adelaide Buckley. Given the way they had parted, he would never have expected to find her in his bed. She hadn't seemed interested, at all.

He stepped in and closed the door.

***

When Henry entered his cabin, Louisa came out of the other room, dressed for bed, in a floor length nightgown.

"Where have you been?" she asked. "I've been worried."

"Turns out you had good reason," he said. "Clint caught two men setting sticks of dynamite down below deck."

"Dynamite? Oh my God. Were they trying to sink

us?"

"They were tryin' to incapacitate us," Henry said. "We would've been dead in the water until we made repairs."

"And probably lost our passengers in Vicksburg," she said. "But it could have sunk us, Henry."

"Yes, it could have," he said.

There was a knock on the door.

"Who's that at this hour?"

"I ordered some coffee from the galley."

He opened the door, accepted the tray of coffee from a crewman, and closed it.

"Why coffee at this hour?" Louisa asked.

"Because you and me," he said, setting in on the table, "we've got to make a list."

THIRTY

"I'm impressed," Adelaide said.

"By what?"

"The fact that you're reading Dumas."

"I thought maybe you were impressed by the simple fact that I read," Clint said.

"Not at all," she said. "I'd never judge you by your reputation. I always judge by what I observe."

"And what is that?"

"You appear to be an intelligent man," she said. "I don't know what kind of formal education you've had, but you certainly seem to be able to fit into any social situation."

"Including this one?"

"Oh yes," she said, drawing her knees up to her chest, "especially this one."

She was covered by the bedsheet, and her shoulders were bare, so he could only assume that, beneath the sheet, she was naked.

"I'm also surprised."

"By what?"

"Finding you here," Clint said. "You didn't seem... interested when we were at the bar."

"Well, that was the point," she said. "To surprise you. Pleasantly, I hope."

"Oh yes," he said, "very pleasantly."

She leaned back against the bedpost, allowing the sheet to slide down a bit, revealing an expanse of creamy, naked breast.

"I saw you with a woman," she said, "the other day. Are you...involved?"

"No," he said, "not involved. She's a friend, a guest on the boat."

"Not a lover?"

"I didn't say that," he said, "but I wouldn't call it a... relationship. In fact, at the moment she's not even speaking to me."

"What a shame," she said. "Something you said or did?"

"Both, I suppose," he answered, "or maybe neither. I can never tell with women."

"Oh, don't try to tell me you don't know how to handle females," she said.

"Let's just say it's a person-by-person thing," he said.

"But there's no chance she'll appear at the door in the next, say, few hours?"

"I doubt it."

"Well then," she said, "you're wasting time." And the sheet dropped again, this time to her waist. Her breasts were well rounded, firm looking, topped with large, pink nipples.

"Yes, I am," he agreed.

***

"Only three names?" Henry asked his wife.

Louisa looked at him from across the table. Her eyes were sleepy.

"You're too trusting, my love," she said. "I can see why you trust Byron, he's been with you so long. Also

Robespierre, because he's the cook and has too much invested in you and the Queen."

"That's only two," Henry said.

"All right," she said, stifling a yawn, "maybe I only trust two men. If you're asking me who I trust now on the boat, then I'd add Clint."

Henry looked down at the piece of paper he'd written six names on. He'd included Byron Stanhope and Terry Robespierre, and four others, but not Clint.

"I don't think Clint meant for us to put his name here," he said.

"Fine," she said. "You have a list of six men?"

"Yes?"

"Then can we go to bed now?"

"You can," he said. "I want to look at this list a little longer."

She stood up, came around to his side of the table, and kissed him.

"Good-night," she said. "Don't stay up too much longer."

"I won't."

When she got to the door she turned and said, "I'm shocked that I'm so sleepy after someone tried to blow us up."

"It's not gonna happen again," he assured her, then thought to himself, at least, not tonight.

***

Byron Stanhope was incensed.

As First Mate he should have Henry Morgan's complete trust. But because Clint Adams happened to be in the right place at the right time...

Who was he kidding? If that dynamite had gone off

and blown a hole in the hull of the Natchez Queen, he would have felt completely responsible. Clint Adams saved him from that. He should thank the man. And yet...

He was seated in his cabin with his big hand wrapped around a bottle of rotgut whiskey. But he hadn't taken a drink, yet. He corked the bottle and pushed it away. This was not the time to get drunk. This was the time to be thinking clearly.

Now that he knew Bill Grant had been one of the saboteurs, he should be able to figure out who the other one was. Or the other ones. Or if not, he should be able to find somebody who could tell him who Grant was close to.

He wasn't going to do anybody any good sitting here in his cabin. With one last look at the bottle of whiskey, he stood up and stomped to the door. When he opened it he stopped short, staring at the man in the hall.

"What are you doin' here?" he asked.

"I gotta talk to you, First Mate," Carl Tobin said. "It's important."

"So talk!"

THIRTY-ONE

Clint removed his gunbelt, walked around the bed while Adelaide watched, and hung it on the bedpost.

"You do that like it's second nature," she said.

"It is," he said, unbuttoning his shirt. "No matter where I am or what I'm doing, this gun has to be within arm's reach."

"Even in bed?"

"Bed, bath tub, whatever," Clint said, removing the shirt. "I never know when somebody's going to take a shot at me."

"I guess I should be nervous, then."

He didn't tell her that she should be more nervous about dynamite than bullets.

She watched, very calmly and serenely, while he removed his boots and the rest of his clothes, until he was standing by the bed naked.

"Very impressive," she said, staring at his hardening cock, but not reaching for it.

Instead, she simply grasped the sheet and tossed it back so that she was now fully exposed. She was very pale, her skin almost translucent, her pale pink nipples beginning to harden. Between her legs was a patch of hair as black—or blacker—than the hair on her head.

"You better get in this bed with me now," she said. "We're wasting time."

THE GUNSMITH #417 - ACE HIGH
***

The First Mate, Byron Stanhope, was shocked.

He stared down at the blood coming from his stomach wound, then at the man holding the knife.

Carl Tobin had stepped inside, and as soon as he closed the door, turned and stuck his knife in Stanhope's stomach.

"What the—" Byron said, clutching at his gut.

"Sorry, Byron," Tobin said, "nothin' personal. I had to do something to make up for the dynamite not going off."

Byron's legs went out from under him and he fell to his knees, still holding his stomach.

Tobin leaned over, so that he was now eye to eye with the First Mate.

"I had to do somethin' that would cripple the Captain, and killin' you filled the bill. He'll be lost without his Mate."

Byron reached out with his left hand, while still holding his stomach with his right. The wound was rapidly robbing him of his strength, so Tobin was able to swat the hand away effortlessly.

He wiped his knife clean on the First Mate's shirt, then pulled a chair over and sat.

"Since the dynamite ploy failed," he said, "I'll have to sit here and wait for you to die. Just to be sure."

"Goddamn you—"

The First Mate fell forward, onto his face, but was not dead, yet.

Tobin leaned down even further.

"By the way," he said, "thanks for signin' me on back in New Orleans."

There was no answer. He checked Byron, found that

he was dead.

"Let's see what they think of this," he said, standing up and moving toward the door.

***

As Clint slid onto the bed next to Adelaide, her hand went down between his legs and took hold of him. He put his arms around her and kissed her mouth, softly, tasting her while she tasted him. When they both decided they liked what they were tasting, the kisses became deeper, longer, and wetter.

After a little while, and as she kept stroking him, he started kissing her neck, shoulders, breasts, working his way to those pink nipples, sucking them into his mouth, biting them, giving them all the attention he felt they deserved before moving on.

"Where are you going?" she asked, as his cock slid from her grasp.

"You'll find out."

He slid down so he could kiss her belly. From there he could smell her, knew that she was wet and ready. Moving his hand over her pubic patch he liked the way it felt against his palm. He delved into the hair with his fingers, found her wet pussy and slid his fingertips along the lips. She gasped and tensed and he delved deeper, getting his fingers very wet. He withdrew them and, meeting her eyes, lifted them first to his nose so he could smell her, and then to his mouth so he could lick them clean.

"Mmmm," he said.

"Jesus," she said, watching as he dipped his head down between her legs. When his tongue touched her she gasped again and moaned, "Oh God..."

THE GUNSMITH #417 - ACE HIGH
***

Tobin went up to the deck, looked around, made sure he was alone. He stood staring out at the water, at the shore and, carefully, lit a cigarette, then drew on it so that the tip glowed brightly. He held it out in front of him.

On the shore a light suddenly appeared, blinked, and then went out.

Tobin flicked his cigarette out into the Mississippi.

Without Grant, he was going to have to press somebody else into service—but not until tomorrow. Not until the body of the First Mate was found, and all the excitement from that calmed down.

And probably not until after the Vicksburg stop. The hole in the hull would have put that off, but now it would probably happen on schedule.

He heard someone in the darkness, walking on the deck, so he turned and to the door he'd come out of and went back below. It was time to return to his own bunk and wait for things to liven up in the morning.

THIRTY-TWO

In the morning Clint woke with Adelaide down between his legs. His cock was in her mouth, already hard. She sucked him wetly, taking him deep, riding him with her wet mouth until he had to lift his butt off the bed as he exploded into that hot, wet mouth...

***

"What's your day going to be like today?" Adelaide asked, as they got dressed.

"Breakfast with the captain," Clint said. "We have some business to take care of."

"What kind of business?" she asked. "Gambling?"

"Some," he said. "We need to talk about Vicksburg."

Adelaide turned and looked at him, fully dressed now. If not for her messy hair, she would have looked perfect.

"Is there something you're not telling me?"

"Probably," he said.

"What's going on?"

"Just some problems that need to be addressed," Clint said. "I may be able to tell you more, later."

"When we know each other better?"

"Yes, when we know each other a little better."

"Well," she said, "I have to go back to my room to

get cleaned up and some clean clothes. Then I want some breakfast, too."

She walked to him as he was pulling on his boots and kissed him.

"I have one request."

"What's that?"

"Not a word to anyone about this," she said. "Not yet."

"All right."

"Not to your friend the Captain."

"Whatever you say."

"As far as anyone in the dining room will know, we saw each other last night at the poker table, and that's all."

"Got it."

"You don't have a problem with that?"

"No." He headed for the door. "What about you?" he asked.

"What do you mean?"

"Who are you going to tell?"

"I don't know anybody sboard," she said. "Who would I tell? My waiter?"

"Okay, then. I'll see you later, for poker."

"Last night was wonderful," she said, at the door, smiling.

"This morning wasn't bad, either," he said.

She laughed and went out the door.

He hadn't told her about the dynamite because he didn't want to worry her. That fact was going to stay with Captain Henry Morgan, the First Mate, and Clint. At least, until they got to Vicksburg and told the law.

Fully dressed, he left the cabin and headed for the dining room.

J.R. ROBERTS
***

Clint found Henry waiting for him at the Captain's table.

"Where's Louisa?" he asked.

"Having breakfast in our cabin. And Charlotte?"

"I haven't seen Charlotte since yesterday," Clint said, sitting.

The waiter appeared immediately and took their orders, providing coffee.

"I've got that list," Henry said. "Louisa and me, we worked on it last night."

"Good." Clint reached out and accepted it. Right at the top were the First Mate and the cook. The other four he didn't recognize.

"Why are the top two names in capital letters?" he asked.

"Because those are the two Louisa and I agree on," Henry said. "I trust the other four, but she doesn't."

"Why not?"

"Well, for one thing, she doesn't know them as well as I do," Henry said. "But they're part of my original crew."

"All right," Clint said. "I'll talk to the First Mate, and tell him I want to meet with these other five men."

"Why?" Henry said. "I told you I trust them."

"And If you trust them, then I want to hear what they think about the whole situation," Clint said. "Maybe they'll know something we don't."

"Oh," Henry said. "Okay."

"How soon before we reach Vicksburg?" Clint asked.

"We'll be there this afternoon."

"Good."

The waiter came with their food. Clint attacked his,

realizing how hungry he was after all the frenzied exercise he'd gotten with Adelaide.

"What do you think the law will do?" Henry asked.

"Truthfully? Not much. They'll take the body, but the murder happened out on the river, not in Vicksburg. They're not going to want to get involved in an investigation."

"So they won't keep us there very long?"

"Probably not."

They were finishing their food when a crew member burst through the doors and hurried to the captain's table. Clint could see that it was all the man could do not to run.

"Captain!"

"What is it, Earl?"

Clint assumed this was Earl Butler, whose name was on Henry's list.

"Sir, you better come."

"Where?"

"It's the first mate, sir," Earl said. "His cabin."

"Earl, calm down."

"I can't!" Earl said, his eyes looking wild. "Captain... the First Mate...he's dead!"

THIRTY-THREE

Clint and Henry Morgan followed the crewman, Earl, to Byron Stanhope's cabin. The First Mate was lying on the floor in a huge pool of blood.

"Jesus," Henry said, but he didn't move from the doorway. Or, more specifically, he couldn't.

Clint stepped into the room, trying not to trod on the bloody mess, but it was difficult if he wanted to check the body. There were no other footprints in the blood. He looked at Earl.

"You didn't check him?"

"No, sir."

"You just assumed he was dead?"

"Ain't he?"

"He is."

"Geez..."

Clint looked at Henry, who still wasn't ready to move or speak.

"Earl," Clint said, "you can go. Not a word to anyone."

"The crew should know—"

"The Captain will tell them," Clint said. "It's not your place to do that."

"Yeah, okay."

"You can go," Clint said.

Earl looked at Henry.

"Go," he said.

"Yes, sir."

He slipped out into the hallway and was gone.

"Henry."

No answer.

"Henry!"

"Yeah?"

"Get inside and close the door."

The Captain moved into the room slowly, closed the door behind him.

Clint couldn't help getting blood on his boots as he checked to see how Byron had been killed.

"Wha-what happened to him?"

"He was stabbed," Clint said, "in the stomach." He stood up. "He must have answered his door and took the knife in the gut."

The captain stared in horror.

"Come on, Henry. Snap out of it."

"My friend is dead."

"Yes, he is."

"But...why?"

"Because we kept the dynamite from going off," Clint said. "So the saboteur had to make another move. This was it."

"So-so what do we do now?"

"This is something else we have to talk to the law in Vicksburg about."

"Yeah, but—no, I mean...what do we do right now?"

"Let's just cover him up," Clint said. "That's all we can do."

"I'll need to let one or two crewmen in on this," Henry said.

"You've already got Earl," Clint said.

"Yeah," Henry said, staring at the body of his First

J.R. ROBERTS

Mate. "One more should do it. We'll need them to carry the bodies off the boat."

"I'm sure the local law in Vicksburg will be able to help with that," Clint said.

He walked into the bedroom, stripped the sheet off the bed, came back and laid it over the body. That seemed to help Henry some with the situation. He took a deep breath.

"We better lock up," Clint said.

"Yeah, right," Henry said.

They left the cabin and locked it behind them.

"Henry," Clint said, as they walked down the hall, "I'm sorry about your friend."

"Yeah," Henry said, "uh, thanks."

They didn't speak again until they were up on deck. Several crewmen and passengers walked past them, greeted them with nods or waves.

"Doesn't look like the word's gotten out," Clint said. "That's good."

"So far," Henry said. "Look, I'm gonna have to tell Louisa what happened."

"Of course."

"And after Vicksburg," he went on, "I'll have to name a new first nate."

"That's up to you," Clint said.

Henry looked out at the water. "This is...this is too much," he said. "I didn't expect this."

"It's too late to change your mind now, Henry."

"Change my mind?"

"About fighting for your boat," Clint said. "Your first mate died for it. You have to keep going."

Henry looked at Clint, then back out at the water, again, shaking his head.

But he said, "You're right If I give up now, Byron

139

died for nothin'."

"That's right."

Henry turned to face Clint.

"Thank you, Clint."

"You better go be with your wife, Henry," Clint said.

"What are you gonna do?"

"I don't know," Clint said. "Walk around, talk to the crew, see who was where."

"Without tellin' them why?"

"If I can," Clint said. "There's nothing else to do until we get to Vicksburg."

"Then use Earl," Henry said, "and he'll tell you who else knows about Byron."

"Okay," Clint said, "I'll find him."

THIRTY-FOUR

Talking to the crew yielded nothing for Clint. It was useless, without telling them why he was asking them the questions he was asking them. So any further investigation would have to wait until after they reached Vicksburg, and the word got out.

As they approached the port, Clint found Henry up on the bridge, in the wheelhouse.

"Did you talk to Louisa?" he asked.

"Yeah," Henry said. "She's very upset. She didn't like Byron very much, but she trusted him. Now she's worried about who's left to trust."

"You and me, I guess," Clint said.

"And Robespierre," Henry said.

"Oh yeah," Clint said, "the cook, and beermaker."

"Right."

Clint looked ahead, saw the port of Vicksburg coming into view.

"How do we do this?" Henry asked.

"I was going to ask you that," Clint said. "How do we get word to the sheriff's office, or police department, or whatever they have in Vicksburg, these days?"

"Through the dockmaster, I guess," Henry said.

"Okay," Clint said, "then when we dock, I'll go and talk to him, get him to send word to the law."

"And do we let people disembark?" Henry asked.

"No," Clint said, "the killer might get off."

"How do I keep them on?"

"Tell them the dockmaster has ordered that nobody leave the boat."

"They'll ask why."

"And tell them you don't know," Clint said, "and you're asking the same question. When you find out you'll let them know."

"And what about passengers who are getting on?" Henry asked. "If there are any."

"You can let them on, I suppose," Clint said. "Why not? They didn't do anything."

"No, they didn't." He slapped the pilot on the back. "Take us in nice and easy, Andy."

"Yes, sir."

"I better get the men ready to carry the bodies off," Henry said to Clint.

"Go!" Clint said.

As Henry left the wheelhouse, Andy looked at Clint and asked, "Bodies?"

Clint wouldn't have told him, except they were almost in port and, before long, everyone would know. Besides, the pilot was one of the men Henry trusted.

"Something happened last night..." he started.

***

When they docked, Clint was the only one to disembark. He made his way to the dockmaster's office and introduced himself.

"Good God," Ambrose Hanson, the dockmaster said, "you've had an eventful trip up our river."

"Yes, we have."

"I know Captain Morgan," Hanson said, "and his first

mate. I'm sorry to hear this. Of course, I'll send someone to fetch the police right away."

"Is it a police department we'll be dealing with?" Clint asked.

"Oh yes," Hanson said, "Vicksburg has had a proper police department for quite some time, now."

"How fast do you think we can get them here?" Clint asked.

"With two bodies?" the dockmaster asked. "Pretty quick."

"Okay," Clint said. "I'll be waiting on the Queen."

"Are you lettin' anybody off?"

"No," Clint said. "The killer might get off."

"And passengers wantin' to get on?"

"We can do that."

"What about loading and unloading cargo?"

"I'll have to ask Captain Morgan if he has any."

"All right," the dockmaster said. "When the police get here I'll come aboard with them."

"Good idea," Clint said. "I'll see you later."

***

Back on the Natchez Queen, Clint told Henry Morgan about his conversation with the dockmaster.

"We have no cargo goin' on or off at this stop," Henry said. "Only passengers. They're already complainin' about not bein' able to disembark."

"Probably because they see people getting on," Clint said.

"Yeah, well, when the police come on board the secret will be out," Henry said.

"Where are the bodies?"

"We've got them wrapped up and ready to be removed," Henry said.

They leaned on the wooden railing of the boat and stared down at the dock. Passengers who were waiting to disembark were doing the same and shouting complaints at Captain Morgan. Passengers who were getting on—and there were only a few—were being shown to their cabins, curious expressions on their faces.

Before long they saw the dockmaster approaching, followed by several policeman in uniforms.

"Here we go," Henry said. "I guess it's time to do some explainin'."

"Let's just talk to the police first," Clint said, "and then you can give your passengers an explanation."

"Good idea."

They went to meet the dockmaster and policemen who were coming up the gangplank.

THIRTY-FIVE

The dockmaster introduced Captain Morgan and Clint Adams to the three policemen, Officers Ramsey, Meeks and Allan. Clint thought they could have been brothers, all in their thirties, and six feet. The Vicksburg police probably had strict standards.

"There is also a detective on the way," Officer Ramsey said.

"And what will you do in the meanwhile?" Henry asked.

"We need to see the bodies," Officer Meeks said.

"That's not a problem," Henry said.

"And we'll need to talk to the people onboard," Officer Allan said.

"You don't know who the killers are, is that correct?" Officer Ramsey asked.

"Partially true," Clint said.

"What do you mean?"

"I killed the first man," Clint said.

"Why?"

"He was sabotaging the boat," Clint said. "He was about to set off two sticks of dynamite. I had no choice."

"And the other body?"

"He was my first mate," Henry said. "We don't know who killed him, but we assume it was one of the saboteurs."

145

THE GUNSMITH #417 - ACE HIGH

"All right," Officer Ramsey said. He seemed to be in charge—at least, until the detective appeared. "Let's see the bodies, and then we can start questioning your passengers and crew."

"This way," Henry said.

As two of the officers followed him, Ramsey turned to Clint and asked, "Are you coming?"

"No," Clint said, "I think I'll wait here for the detective. Since I killed one of the men, I'm sure he'll want to talk to me."

"Sir, you're the Gunsmith, is that correct?"

"It is."

"Mr. Adams," Ramsey said, "I'd really prefer it that you don't leave the boat."

"I have no intention of leaving, Officer Ramsey," Clint said. "After all, it was me who sent for you."

"Yes," Ramsey said, "of course." He started away, then looked down at the dock and stopped. "Well, it seemed you won't have to wait long."

"What's that?"

"Detective Halloran is here." Ramsey pointed.

Clint looked down to see a man in a suit and a bowler hat starting up the gangplank.

"Well, that's good," he said. "Can you introduce us?"

"Yes, of course," Ramsey said.

***

After Ramsey introduced Clint and Halloran he went below deck to join his colleagues in looking at the bodies.

"Well, this is a real pleasure," Halloran said. "Meeting the Gunsmith. I just wish it was under other circumstances."

146

"So do I, Detective." The man was in his forties, had a presence that hinted at competence. Clint hoped he was reading him right.

"Why don't you fill me in on what's been happening?" the detective asked.

Clint told him why he was on board, what had happened the night before with the dynamite, and then what had been discovered just that morning.

"I'd like to see the cabin where the First Mate was killed," Halloran said.

"Sure, I'll take you down."

Clint led the man below decks, to Byron Stanhope's cabin. He stood aside and watched while the detective surveyed the scene. The blood had pooled in the center of the floor. A large space outlined where the body had lain.

"So," he said, finally, "do you or the Captain have any ideas about who the killer might be?"

"No," Clint said. "I had the Captain make a list of the people he absolutely trusted on board."

"And how many were there?"

"Six," Clint said, "but Stanhope was one of them, and now he's dead."

"So that leaves five," Halloran said. "As far as the Captain is concerned, everyone else is a suspect."

"Yes."

"Even the passengers."

"Oh, yes."

"Well," the detective said, "I assume my men are questioning everyone."

"But how long can we keep people from leaving?" Clint asked.

"Not very long," Halloran said. "My men and I are here as a courtesy, Mr. Adams."

"What do you mean?"

"This crime took place on the river," Halloran said, "not in Vicksburg. We can't detain anybody here."

"What about getting on the boat with us?" Clint asked.

"I can't do that."

"Why not?"

"Once I leave Vicksburg," Halloran said, "I don't have any authority."

"So then who does?"

"That's a question I can't answer," Halloran said. "I'm guessing you'd need some Federal help."

"So a Marshal?"

"That'd be my guess."

"And what do we do in the meantime?"

"While you're docked, I'll do my best to find out what happened,"

Halloran said.

"Then we might as well get to it," Clint said.

THIRTY-SIX

The three uniformed policemen questioned the passengers and crew, Clint stayed with Detective Halloran while he questioned Clint's colleagues who ran games in the salon.

"Why them?" Clint asked him.

"Why not?" Halloran replied. "Did you think your saboteur could only come from the passengers or crew?"

The news of Byron Stanhope's murder was an apparent shock to most people. Some of them got angry about it, some just got upset. Henry, Clint and the police decided not to tell the others about the dynamite.

Lockhart was someone who didn't get angry, and also didn't seem all that upset.

"That's a shame," was all he said.

They were questioning Lockhart right in the salon, while he sat at his empty table.

"You don't seem all that upset," Halloran observed, "or surprised to hear that the first mate was killed."

"Well," Lockhart said, "I deal poker, I don't work out on deck with the first mate, so I didn't know him all that well. It's a shame that he's dead, but..." He shrugged.

"That's a little cold, Mr. Lockhart," the detective said, "even if you didn't know him."

Lockhart looked annoyed.

"Detective," he said, "if I didn't know him very

well it stands to reason I also had no reason to kill him. Doesn't that follow?"

"Possibly."

"I'm sorry somebody killed him," the dealer said, "but it really doesn't affect me. Unless it puts this boat into dry dock."

"That's not up to me."

"Well then, if there's nothing else," Lockhart said, "I'll get back to my solitaire."

Clint wanted to say something, but he decided to save it for later. They were finished in the salon, so they stepped outside.

"I'm going to go and talk to my men," Halloran said, "and see what we've got."

"Okay," Clint said. "I'll go and find the captain. We'll be on the deck."

"We'll talk," Halloran promised, and the two men split up.

***

Clint found captain henry Morgan on the deck and joined him at the rail.

"What do you think?" Henry asked.

"I don't think we've got anything," Clint said. "The police are going to let the passengers go."

He explained Halloran's reasoning to Henry, who stood there, shaking his head.

"So we have to solve this ourselves?"

"Or," Clint said, "have a federal marshal waiting for us when we get to St. Louis."

"But the passengers will be gone by then," Henry said.

"To tell you the truth," Clint said, "I don't think

we're looking at a passenger, I think we're looking for a crew member."

"I hate to hear that," Henry said, "but I agree."

"And if there is a saboteur among the passengers," Clint went on, "then that passenger isn't getting off here until he's done his job."

"I'm glad you're here, Clint," Henry said, "because I'm just not thinkin' straight."

Clint slapped Henry on the back and said, "I don't blame you, my friend. You're trying to hang onto your boat, and you've lost a friend."

They both turned as Detective Halloran came back, leading the three policemen.

"What's the verdict?" Clint asked the detective.

"You had crewmen who liked your first mate, and crewmen who didn't like him, but I can't say whether one of them killed him or not. As for the passengers, I can't see why any of them would have had a motive. Unless one of them actually came on your boat to do the job."

"So it's time to let the passengers disembark?" Henry asked.

"I'm afraid so," Halloran said. "There's not much more that we can do."

"Well," Henry said, "I appreciate the time you spent on board, Detective. You and your men."

"I wish we could have done more, sir."

The uniformed policemen stationed themselves at the top and bottom of the gang plank, in the event they might hear or see something as people left the boat.

The detective remained on the deck with Clint and Henry.

"If I could, I'd stay on the boat with you, Captain," Halloran said. "But you've got the Gunsmith here. He's a legend."

"I know that, Detective."

Henry went to talk to a few crew members who had gathered together and were grumbling. He knew he needed to settle them down before they got under way.

"Mr. Adams," Halloran said, "my advice is not to look for someone with a personal grudge. I think you've got some muscle for hire on this boat, and they're part of the crew, not the passenger list."

That was what Clint had been thinking, too, but he said, "Thanks for the advice, Detective. I appreciate it."

The two men shook hands and Detective Halloran joined his three men, who were now down on the dock.

"This was not a good stop," Henry said. "My crew's grumbling, the passengers aren't happy, we don't know who was settin' the dynamite, and we sure as hell don't know who killed Byron."

"You better make whatever arrangements you need to make to get your boat underway, Henry," Clint said. "I think the only place we're going to get answers to our questions is out on that river."

THIRTY-SEVEN

They finished loading and offloading passengers and the Natchez Queen pulled away from the Vicksburg dock. Clint watched the dock disappear behind them from the bridge.

"Here," Henry said.

Clint looked at the man standing beside him, who was holding out a bottle to him. There was no label on it.

"What is it?"

"Robespierre's beer."

"Okay, then." Clint took it and had a healthy swig, then handed it back. "How's the crew?"

"Unhappy," Henry said. "Crabby. Whether they liked Byron or not, they're not happy that somebody killed him."

"What about the passengers?"

"The new ones want to gamble," Henry said. "Apparently, they heard about you."

"How many did we get?"

"Six or seven."

"And the old ones?"

"They're shocked that there was a murder on board, but they didn't know Byron, so there's no personal reaction."

"What about Charlotte?" Clint asked.

"What about her?"

"Have you talked to her?" Clint asked. "Did the police? I haven't seen her in over a day."

"She must really be mad at you."

"Yeah," Clint said, "or maybe there's another reason."

"Like what?" Henry asked. "Wait, do you think she's workin' with the saboteurs?"

"I don't know what to think," Clint said. "Has Louisa seen her?"

"I'll have to ask."

"Where is she now?"

"My cabin."

"Let's go down there and talk to her," Clint said, "and then check on Charlotte."

"Okay," Henry said. He took a last drink from the bottle, emptying it. "Let's go."

***

When they entered Henry and Louisa's cabin, she was sitting at the table, fully dressed, and looked up at them.

"How's everything going?" she asked.

Henry walked to her and kissed her.

"We're underway," he said. "Clint has a question for you."

"What is it?" she asked, looking at Clint.

"It's about Charlotte," Clint said. "Have you talked to her, or seen her today?"

"No, I haven't."

"And not yesterday?" Clint asked.

"Come to think of it," Louisa said, "no. Is there something wrong?"

"We don't know," Clint said, "but we're going to

check."

***

They left Henry's cabin, telling Louisa they'd let her know immediately if something was wrong. They went to Charlotte's cabin and knocked on the door several times.

"She's not in," Henry said.

"Or she is and something's wrong."

"Well, we didn't see her on deck at all," Henry said. "Shall I open it?"

"Do you have a key?"

"I have a key that fits all the cabins," Henry said. "It's my boat."

Henry took the key out and unlocked the door. They stepped inside, careful to close the door behind them.

"Charlotte!" Clint called.

No answer.

"Charlotte!" he called again. "It's Clint."

Still no answer.

Henry looked in the bedroom.

"She's not in there, and the bed is made."

Clint looked around the room.

"What strikes you about this room?"

Henry looked around.

"It's neat."

"It's more than that," Clint said. "It's not lived in."

"You mean she hasn't used it?"

"That's what I mean."

"So she's been sleepin'...with you?"

"No."

Clint walked around, then peered into the bedroom. Charlotte's suitcases were there, as well as her trunk.

THE GUNSMITH #417 - ACE HIGH

Clint walked over to the trunk, opened it, pawed through it, then stopped and stared.

"Henry! You better come see this."

Henry joined him in the bedroom.

"Oh my God."

They were looking at several more sticks of dynamite, nestled among some of Charlotte's dresses and underthings.

"I wondered where they could have been hiding dynamite onboard," Henry said.

"They weren't," Clint said. "She brought it with her."

"She's workin' with them."

"And she used me to get onboard," Clint said, angrily.

"Don't take the blame for that," Henry said. "She had already paid for passage."

"She did?"

Henry nodded.

"Why didn't you tell me?"

"You wanted her to be your guest," Henry said. "I was gonna return her passage money."

"Well," Clint said, still looking at the dynamite, "before you can do that, we'll have to find her, first."

THIRTY-EIGHT

They'd have to search the boat to try and locate Charlotte, but first they went back to Louisa to tell her what they discovered.

"Dynamite?" Louisa said. "In her luggage? Oh my God."

"I know," Henry said.

"We were making friends," she said. "she was so nice."

"When she wasn't trying to turn you against your husband," Clint reminded her.

"Oh my God," Louisa said, again. "That was part of the sabotage. She wanted to drive a wedge between us."

"That's what I was thinking," Clint said.

Suddenly, Louisa was angry.

"That bitch!"

"That's what I was thinking," her husband said.

"I'll tear her hair out," Louisa said.

"We have to find her, first," Clint said. "She's not in her cabin."

"Is she even om board?"

"She didn't get off," Clint said. "Nobody got off while we weren't watching."

"So then she's hiding," Louisa said. "She can't be hiding from us on our own boat." She looked at her husband. "We can find her."

157

"Unless," Clint said, "somebody's hiding her."

"The crew?" Henry asked. "You think one of the crew is hiding her in his bunk?"

"Do any of the crew have their own cabin?" Clint asked.

"No," Henry said.

"Henry..." Louisa said. "You gave Robespierre his own cabin."

"The cook?" Clint asked.

"He can't be part of this," Henry said.

"There's one way to find out, Henry," Clint said. "Let's go to his cabin first."

"I want to come," Louisa said. "I want to give her a piece of my mind."

"I think you better stay here, Louisa," Clint said. "It'll be safer."

"But—"

"He's right," Henry said. "Don't worry. When we find her, we'll give you a chance to talk to her."

"You better!" Louisa said.

***

They left the Captain's cabin and made their way to the crew's deck.

"The first mate was supposed to be the only crew member with his own cabin," Henry explained, "but Louisa's right, I gave the cook his own, because—"

"He's a good cook..."

"Well, yeah, but—"

". . . and he makes great beer."

"Yep, that, too."

They reached the cabin door and Henry knocked.

No answer.

"Terry!" Henry called out, knocking again.

"Guess he's in the kitchen," Clint said.

"We'll go there and see him," Henry said.

"Or we could go in and have a quick look around his cabin," Clint said. "Maybe Charlotte's in there."

Henry hesitated.

"All you have to do is use your key."

Henry took out his skeleton key.

"Is there another way out of there?" Clint asked.

"No."

Henry put the key in the lock and opened the door.

"I'll go first," Clint said.

Henry didn't argue. He still didn't think the cook could be involved, so he was reluctant to go into the cabin. He didn't want to find anything that would prove him wrong.

Clint entered the one room cabin, took it in with a quick glance around. Charlotte was not there, and it didn't look as if she had ever been.

"Come on in, Henry," Clint said. "It's empty."

Henry walked in and stopped just inside the door. Looking around, he seemed relieved.

"She's not here."

"No," Clint said, walking in a circle, "and it doesn't look like she ever has been."

"So now what?"

"Where else could a crew member be hiding her?"

"The rest of the crew sleep in bunks," Henry said. "There's no way one of them could be hiding her."

"Well," Clint said, "not in their bunk, anyway."

"Below decks," Henry said, "where we keep the cargo and livestock. She could be there."

"Then I guess that's where we're going to have to look," Clint said.

THE GUNSMITH #417 - ACE HIGH

They left the cabin and Henry locked the door.

"You think a lady like Charlotte would hide out down there?" Henry asked in the hall.

"Well maybe," Clint replied, "she's not as much of a lady as we all first thought. I mean, what kind of a lady hides dynamite in with her underwear?"

"That's a good point," Henry said.

THIRTY-NINE

First they went below deck to look in among the cargo to see if Charlotte was hiding behind any crates. There were two crew members down there to help them. They snapped to attention when they saw the captain.

"My friend has some questions," Henry told them. "Tell him whatever he wants to know."

"Yes sir."

"Clint, this is Lew, and this is Benny."

The two crew members, probably in their 40's, looked as if they'd been traveling the river for a long time.

"We're looking for a woman," Clint said, "hiding somewhere on the boat."

Lew and Benny exchanged a glance.

"We were wondering if you've seen a woman down here," Clint said. "She a big woman, very beautiful. You can't miss her."

"There's a woman like that who's a passenger," Lew said.

"Yeah, we all saw her," Henny said.

"Well, that's who we're looking for," Clint said. "We know she's involved in the recent sabotage on the ship, and now she's hiding from us."

"She ain't down here," Lew said.

"Ain't seen her down here," Benny said.

161

THE GUNSMITH #417 - ACE HIGH

Clint studied the two men. One or both of them could have been Charlotte's partner. And actually be the one hiding her.

"You're sure?" he asked.

"Like you said," Benny replied, "we couldn't miss her."

Clint wondered which one—if either of them—was lying.

Finally, Clint said to Henry, "We better go and check the livestock and see if she's bedded down in the hay, there."

"A lady?" Lew asked. "There?"

"This lady needs a place to hide," Clint said, "and she might not be choosy."

"You boys spot her, you give us a holler. You hear me?" Captain Morgan said.

"Aye, sir!" both men said.

Clint and Henry left and headed for the livestock area.

***

There was one man there. His name was Tobias, a man in his 50's who seemed to have more tattoos than teeth.

"Naw," he said, "I ain't seen no woman down here in...well, ever! I think it's the smell keeps 'em away."

Clint didn't know if he meant the smell of the animals, or his smell. It could have been either one.

"Okay," Henry said, "if you do see a woman down here, let me know."

"Aye, sir!"

***

Back on deck Henry said to Clint, "And now what?"

"First you're going to have to name your new first mate," Clint said.

"And then?"

":And then you, me and the first mate will come up with some patrols, made up of crew members we trust."

"That may not be so easy," Henry said. "I am findin' myself less and less trustful of my people."

"Still," Clint said. "You have your list."

"Yes."

"So you'll choose your first mate from it?"

"I'll have to."

"Let me know when you've made your choice."

"And until then?"

"I'll deal poker."

"What about the saboteurs?"

"It's our first night out of Vicksburg," Clint said. "I think they'll take their time deciding on their next move."

"Well," Henry said, "I won't take long to decide. I better go to my cabin now and tell Louisa what we found...nothin'!"

Clint patted his friend on the shoulder and said, "We'll keep looking, Henry."

Henry nodded and walked away, leaving Clint there, leaning on the railing and looking out at the passing shoreline.

***

"I can't stay here much longer, Carl!" Charlotte hissed.

Tobin looked at her. Her clothes were in a state of disarray, as was her hair, yet she looked more beautiful, more glorious than he'd ever seen her.

"You're in hiding, Charlotte," he said. "Where else would you go? Back to your cabin?"

"Why not?" she asked. "They've already searched there."

Tobin thought a moment. That might not be such a bad idea, but he stared at her, on her knees on a thin mattress, her breasts spilling out of her dress, and he knew he didn't want her in her cabin, he wanted her right here.

"We can think about that," he said, undoing his trousers. "After."

"After?" She laughed. "You think I'm going to fuck you now? Here? We both stink?"

"You stink of sex," he said, dropping his pants so that his hard cock sprang into view.

Her eyes went right to it and she said, "Damn you!" and reached for him. She pulled him to her and took him into her mouth, proceeded to suck hit wetly until he was good and hard, then she fell onto her back, lifted her skirt and spread her legs.

"Take me then," she said. "Fuck me hard, while we're both still free to do it."

He got on his knees, pressed the head of his cock against the wet lips of her pussy, and then drove himself into her with a gasp of pleasure as her heat engulfed him.

"Oooh, God!" she moaned.

"We're free to do this," he told her, "and more. At least he knew the Gunsmith wasn't fucking her, anymore. That had just been to get him interested. Now she was his, exclusively. Her big beautiful ass, full, gorgeous tits and wet pussy were all his.

FORTY

Clint appeared in the salon that night to play poker, resplendent in his new suit. As he entered, he saw that all the other dealers were in place, as well. The salon seemed busier, with the new passengers they'd picked up in Vicksburg added to the players who were already on board.

He went to his table and had just broken the seal on a fresh deck of cards, when Captain Henry Morgan came in and approached his table.

"I chose my first mate."

"Have I met him?"

"No," Henry said, "but he was on my list. His name's Paul Burkette. He's been with me for three years."

"Okay," Clint said.

"He'll have breakfast with us in the mornin', and we'll talk about patrols."

"Good."

Henry looked over his shoulder.

"Here come a couple of new players, who got on in Vicksburg," he said. "Good luck."

"I thought it looked like a better crowd." Clint smiled.

"Yes, for now," Henry said. "I'm hopin' we pick up a lot more in St. Louis—that is, if we get to St. Louis."

"We'll get there," Clint said. "Now, get lost. Let me play my part."

THE GUNSMITH #417 - ACE HIGH

Henry nodded, and left the table just as the two new passengers—both men—reached the table.

"Are you the Gunsmith?" one of them asked.

"That's right," Clint said. "Interested in a game?"

"Oh yes," the other man said, his eyes bright with excitement.

These two, Clint thought, weren't going to be any trouble, at all.

***

The men played for hours, lost heavily, but didn't seem to mind. Apparently, they both had a lot of money and were willing to pay for the experience of playing with the Gunsmith.

Along the way several other players came, lost and went. None of them were professional players. Clint found that he didn't even have to fully concentrate to beat them. That meant his mind could wander, to a certain degree.

Clint hadn't really expected to encounter professional poker players on the Natchez Queen, but he wondered what St. Louis would bring aboard. Then he thought about what Henry had said, that first they'd have to make it to their next destination.

So far all attempts on the boat had been to incapacitate it, to make Henry unable to carry out his responsibilities. If it kept up, he'd lose his business and, eventually, his boat. But so far no one had tried to destroy it. Someone obviously wanted Henry to lose it, so they could gain it.

***

Clint took a break when the players got down to the original two. The passengers said they'd wait for him at the table.

"Can we keep playing while we wait?" one of them asked.

"Against each other?"

"No!"

So instead they played solitaire, one watching the other.

Clint went to the bar for a beer, but mostly because Henry was standing there with another man.

"Clint, meet Paul Burkette, our new first mate."

"Mr. Adams," Burkette said.

"Mr. Burkette.

"How's your g"ame goin'?" Henry asked.

"Fine," Clint said, "nobody's winning,"

"That's good."

"They're not good players, so I've had time to think about our problem."

"And?"

Clint explained his thoughts to Henry and Burkette, who listened intently.

"So," he finished, "in the past few weeks, or months, has anybody tried to buy the Natchez Queen from you?"

"Actually," Henry said, "I've had two offers in the past month. I turned them both down."

"And the sabotage on the boat?" Clint asked. "Did it start after the first offer was turned down, or the second?"

"The second."

"So it could be one of those prospective buyers who's behind it all."

"That sounds right."

"Or both buyers," Burkette said, "could be workin' together."

"Or," Clint added, "both buyers could be working for the same person."

"Okay, wait, wait," Henry said. "None of this does us any good while we're on board."

"Do you know how to contact the buyers?" Clint asked.

"Yes," Henry said, "they both left me with telegraph addresses."

"What's our next stop?"

"A town called Greenville, Mississippi, and then Memphis."

"How many more stops after that before we hit St. Louis?" Clint asked.

"Let's see...New Madrid, Cape Girardeau, both in Missouri, then Chester, Illinois, before we make St. Louis."

"Okay," Clint said, "so the biggest stop we have before St. Louis is Memphis."

"Right."

"Maybe," Clint said, "we can send a couple of telegrams when we get there."

"Saying what?" Burkette asked.

"We've got some time to figure that out," Clint replied.

FORTY-ONE

The next morning, Clint had breakfast with Henry and the first mate, Burkette.

Once they had their food, Clint looked at Burkette and said, "We need to get something straight."

"Okay."

"The Captain trusts you," Clint said. "I don't know you, so I have to take his word. But if I find out you're the saboteur, or you're working with them—"

"I've been on this boat for three years, Adams," Burkette said. "And I don't know you, either."

"Let's take it easy. The three of us are gonna have to trust each other," Henry said.

Clint and Burkette took their eyes off each other and looked at Henry Morgan.

"Agreed," Clint said.

"Agreed," Burkette said.

"Paul, Clint's in charge of our security, so what he says goes. Understand?"

"Aye, sir," Burkette said. He looked at Clint again. "What are your orders...sir?"

"First," Clint said, "don't call me sir. Just Clint will do. Second, we need to have patrols on the boat."

"So nobody sets any dynamite," Burkette said "Got it. How many men?"

"Two teams of two," Clint said. "Especially at night.

They start at opposite ends from each other, so that they never cross during the night."

"Shouldn't they?" Burkette asked.

"What do you mean?" Henry asked.

"Shouldn't they meet at least once during the night, to compare notes?"

Henry looked at Clint.

"He has a good point," Clint said. "In fact, they should cross paths twice. We'll work that out."

"Okay, fine," Henry said.

"Who do they report to?" Burkette asked.

"To you, Burkette," Clint said.

"And I report to you?"

"That's right," Clint said. "And I'll be in contact with the Captain."

Burkette nodded. "Agreed. When do we start?"

"How quickly can you choose four men you can trust?" Clint asked.

"I can do it today," Burkette said. "We can have the first patrols out tonight."

"That's good," Clint said.

"Is there anything else?"

"Yes," Clint said. "We're still looking for one of our passengers. Charlotte Chandler."

Burkette's eyebrows went up. "I know who that is."

"She seems to be...missing."

"Missin'?"

"Or hidin'," Henry said.

"Which is it?"

"We're not sure," Clint said, "but it seems like she's probably hiding."

"That'll make her hard to find."

"How many places could there be on this boat to hide?" Clint asked.

"Are you kiddin'?" Burkette asked. "A lot."

"Really?" Henry asked.

"Yessir," Burkette said. "The crew has lots of places they use to, uh, hide from you, Cap'n."

"Is that a fact?"

"I'm afraid so, sir."

Henry looked at Clint, who said, "Well, it's not important now why those places exist. We just have to check them."

"I can do a search and use the same four men I'm gonna put on the patrols," Burkette offered.

"Okay," Clint said, "that sounds good. Get it done."

"Yessir," Burkette said. He looked down at the rest of the food on his plate. "Is after breakfast soon enough?"

"Of course," Henry said. "Finish your food, Paul."

"Thank you, sir."

They all finished their food, and then while Clint and Henry had more coffee, Burkette left the dining room to get the search started.

***

Soon after Burkette left, Louisa appeared. She joined Clint and Henry at the table.

"Breakfast?" Henry asked.

"Just coffee," Louisa said, "I'm still too mad to eat."

Henry poured the coffee for his wife.

"What are we doing to find Charlotte?" she asked.

"We're still searching," Clint said. "The new first mate is putting together a search party."

"Burkette?" she asked, looking at Henry. "Did you give him the job?"

"Yes, I did."

"He's one of the men we both agreed on."

"Yes."

She looked at Clint. "What will you do when you have her?"

"Find out who she's working with," Clint said, "or for."

"For?"

Henry told her what Clint had brought up about possible buyers for the boat.

"There were two," she said.

"That's what I told him."

"Um, that fellow...Andrew Hackett," she said. "He already owns several boats and wants to add the Natchez Queen."

"Right, right," Henry said, "and the other one was..."

"...Everett Winston," she said. "His offer came through a bank. Was he a banker?"

"I don't know," Henry said, "I just turned him down."

"Businessmen," Clint said.

"Do businessmen use sabotage to get what they want?" Louisa asked.

"They use whatever they have to use," Clint said. "That's why I haven't liked most of the ones I've met."

"What about those telegrams?" Henry asked.

"What telegrams?" Louisa asked.

"Clint wants me to send a couple of telegrams when we get to Memphis."

"To who?"

"The prospective buyers," Clint said, "Hackett and Winston."

"Saying what?" she asked.

"I haven't figured that out, yet," Clint said.

FORTY TWO

In the afternoon, First Mate Burkette came looking for Clint, found him at the bar in the now empty gambling salon.

"Have a beer," Clint said.

"Crew is not supposed to drink in here," Burkette said. "I just came to talk to you."

"Have a beer," Clint said. "It's okay, you're with me." He waved to the bartender to serve Burkette a cold beer.

"Thanks," Burkette said, and gratefully drank half of it down. "I haven't had good beer in a long time."

"Finish it and have another," Clint said. "We'll go to a table and talk."

Burkette drank it down, then accepted a second from the barman and followed Clint to his poker table, now empty but for a deck of cards.

Clint sat, reached for the deck of cards, held it in his hands while they spoke.

"Why did you need to see me?"

"We've searched," Burkette said, "and we ain't found the woman, Charlotte."

"Keep searching."

"How long?"

"Until it's time for the patrols."

"I thought we'd have day patrols, and night patrols.

Just in case someone tried something during the day."

"That's a good idea," Clint said, "but those same four men can't do both patrols. They need sleep."

"I'll have to find more men."

"The more we use, the more chance we'll be including one of the saboteurs," Clint said.

"I'll pick men I trust."

"How many of the crew do you trust, Burkette?" Clint asked. "When the Captain himself trusts maybe half a dozen?"

"The captain doesn't mix with the men the way I do," Burkette said. "I know there are more than six loyal men on this boat."

"Then why don't you make me a list, Burkette."

"A list of what?" the first mate asked. "Men who can be trusted?"

"No," Clint said, "a list of men you can't trust. It would be shorter, wouldn't it?"

"Yes, I can do that," Burkette said, "and yes, it would be shorter."

Clint studied the man across the table. He was in his mid-forties, and had probably been on the Mississippi many, many years. It meant a lot to him, as did the Natchez Queen.

"All right," Clint said. "Make your list today, start your patrols tonight. Tomorrow we'll start the daylight patrols, as well. You'll tell the Captain and me which men you'll be using."

"Yes, sir," Burkette said, "I'll do that." he pushed his chair back.

"Finish your beer before you go."

Burkette drained his mug, then left the salon.

***

Tobin sat beside Charlotte on the thin mattress.

"I wish you hadn't left the dynamite in your cabin," he told her. "They found it."

"I had no choice."

"Well, now they're searching for you," Tobin said.

"Will they look here?"

"Eventually."

"So what do we do?"

"One of two things."

"Pray tell."

"Well, we can get you off the boat, or we can do something to take their mind off finding you."

"How can you get me off the boat?"

"You could jump off and swim to shore."

"Okay," she said, "what's your next plan?"

"Well," he said, "we damage the boat enough to keep their minds off you."

"We don't have any dynamite. They confiscated what was in my trunk.'"

"I know."

"Then how do we damage the boat?"

"Maybe we don't," he said.

"Now you're talking in riddles."

He turned his head and looked at her.

"Maybe we need to damage some *one*," Tobin said, "rather than some *thing*."

"The captain?"

"I don't think our employer wants him hurt."

"Then who?"

He shrugged.

"Maybe the captain's wife," he said, "maybe his friend, Clint Adams."

"How do you plan on hurting the Gunsmith?"

"I don't know," Tobin said, "but I'll have to come

up with a way quick. The captain has named a new first mate, and he's leading a search party for you."

"Great."

"He's also putting together patrols," Tobin said. "Day and night."

"Then we have to move fast," she said. "Tonight."

"Yeah," Tobin said, "we do."

"What about the others?"

"I'll talk to them," he said, getting up off the mattress. "Stay here until I come back."

"Don't leave me here too long," she said. "I don't want to be found."

"Soon as I can," he promised.

FORTY-THREE

Clint played poker most of the night, noticed across the floor that Ed Lockhart also had some players at his table. Since the extra passengers had come on board, Lockhart had seemed to be in a better mood. At least, he hadn't gotten drunk and staggered over to Clint's table lately.

Looking around the room, though, Clint could see that Henry Morgan's boat was still not doing the business necessary to survive. Maybe their passenger list would increase when they stopped in Memphis, and then again when they hit St. Louis. He hoped so, for his friend's sake.

He also hoped they'd be able to figure out who'd been trying to sabotage the boat, long before either stop.

He played til late into the night, when the last player decided to give up and go to his cabin. Since he wasn't going to be playing anymore, he went to the bar for a beer.

As he accepted his mug from the bartender, Lockhart came walking over to him.

"Mind if I join you?"

"Why not, Ed?"

The bartender gave Lockhart a beer.

"Business has picked up," Lockhart said.

"Not enough, though," Clint answered.

"We've got more stops," the other man said. "Maybe your name will bring them aboard."

"That's Henry's plan."

"You don't think so?"

"I don't know, Ed," Clint said. "I just hope so."

Lockhart finished his beer and set the empty mug on the bar.

"I'm not used to seein' you dressed like this, Adams," he said. "You look like...well, me."

With a wave he was gone from the salon.

"Another one?" the bartender asked.

"I'll just take my time finishing this one," Clint said.

But before he could get it to his mouth again, they heard shots—two of them—and Clint was running for the doors.

***

The deck was dark, as the moon was just a sliver in the sky. Clint stopped and looked around. He heard feet running toward him, then saw two of the men who were on patrol.

"What's going on?" he demanded.

"We don't know," one man said. "We heard shots."

"Not from your way?"

"No."

"Okay, then this way," Clint said, and ran.

They hurried along the deck until they suddenly came upon a figure lying there.

"Damn it!" Clint said.

He stopped, leaned over the body and turned it over.

"Who is it?" one of the men asked.

"Ed Lockhart."

"The dealer?" the other one asked.

"Yes," Clint said. He turned and looked over his shoulder at the two men. "Okay, one of you go and find the captain. The other gather up the other two men on patrol, and then the three of you take a good look around."

"Aye, sir," they both said, and ran off.

Clint leaned over to listen to Lockhart's breathing, but there was nothing to hear. He should have told one of the men to bring him a torch.

His eyes were used to the darkness enough to see the two damp spots on Lockhart's back. The man had been shot from behind. But why? Why shoot Ed Lockhart as a form of sabotage? How would that damage the boat's functions at all?

There was only one answer he could think off.

"What the hell—" he heard, as Henry Morgan came running up. Along with him came Paul Burkette. Both men were holding oil lamps.

"It's Lockhart," Clint said.

"Dead?"

Clint nodded. "Shot in the back."

"But...why?" Burkette asked. "Why kill him? He's not even a member of the crew. How does killing a poker player sabotage the boat, at all?"

"It doesn't," Clint said, "but killing me might."

"Whataya mean?" Burkette asked.

"The last thing Lockhart said to me before he left the salon was that I was dressed like him, which means he was dressed like me."

"So you're sayin'," Henry commented, "that somebody shot him in the back, thinkin' it was you."

"That's what I'm saying," Clint said. "It's the only explanation."

"Where are the patrols?" Burkette asked.

"I sent them to look for you, and the other patrol,"

Clint said. "Then I told them to start searching the deck."

"Okay," Burkette said, "so they're probably all together now."

"We know they have someplace on board to hide that we haven't found yet," Clint said. "Whoever shot Lockhart probably went right there."

"So we're not gonna find them," Burkette said.

"Not tonight, anyway," Henry said.

"Come on," Clint said, "let's carry Lockhart back into the salon."

"And then what?" Burkette asked.

"And then we'll figure out our next move. At least they didn't get done what they think they got done."

"Hey that's right," Henry said, taking the feet while Clint took the shoulders, "they must think you're dead."

FORTY-FOUR

They got Lockhart's body laid out on a table in the saloon. Under the good lighting Clint was able to confirm what he had seen in the dark—two bullet wounds in the back.

"This had to be meant for me," he said to Henry.

He looked around. Aside from himself, Captain Morgan, first mate Burkette and the bartender, no one else was in the room.

"So just the four of us, and the four men on patrol, know that the dead man is not me."

"And you want to keep it that way?" Henry said.

"For now."

Somebody appeared at the door.

"Who's that?" he asked.

"The men on patrol," Burkette said.

"Go and talk to them," Clint said. "See what they've found."

"And if they found nothin'?"

"Have them look again, but leave one of them on that door. We don't want anyone else in here."

"Right."

"Boss?" Henry looked at the bartender who was holding out a white table cloth.

"Yeah, right," Henry said. He took the cloth and spread it out over the dead man.

THE GUNSMITH #417 - ACE HIGH

"You want a drink?" the bartender asked.

"A bottle of whiskey," Henry said, "and three glasses."

"Right."

He took the bottle and glasses from the man and said to Clint, "Let's sit."

Clint noticed that Henry had dressed quickly, hadn't bothered to button the top button of his shirt, or the cuffs, and hadn't combed his hair.

They sat and Henry filled three shot glasses. Burkette joined them, looked surprised, but sat down to join them, anyway.

"So what now?" Henry asked.

"Now we have another murder to report to the law when we dock," Clint said.

"In Greenville?"

"Well," Clint said, "I have a suggestion about that."

"What?"

"Let's skip Greenville and go right to Memphis. It'll have a bigger police presence—probably a police department."

"And they'll probably tell us the same thing the Vicksburg police told us," Henry said, "that they can't help us."

"That's okay," Clint said. "We'll help ourselves."

"And how are we gonna do that?" Burkette asked.

"I'm going to find the sonofabitch who did this!" Clint said.

"I didn't know you and Lockhart were such good friends," Henry said.

"We weren't," Clint said. "That was supposed to be me. I don't take kindly to somebody trying to shoot me in the back."

"And how are we gonna find him?" Henry asked.

"I haven't figured that out yet," Clint said, "but by the time we get to Memphis I'll have a plan."

He pushed his empty glass toward Henry, who refilled it.

***

They decided to move Lockhart's body to a storage area on the boat, cleaned his blood off the table, and closed the salon.

Burkette swore his men to secrecy, but somehow, Clint felt sure the word would get out that he wasn't dead.

He went down to his cabin, feeling bone weary. As he entered, Adelaide Buckley looked at him from the bed. She was not naked, but clad in a filmy nightgown, and reading one of his books, a collection of Mark Twain's short stories.

"You look awful," she said, closing the book. "What happened?"

"Somebody tried to kill me."

"What?"

"They shot Ed Lockhart in the back, thinking it was me," he explained.

"That's awful. Is he dead?"

"Yes."

"Did you catch whoever did it?"

"No," he said, "but we will."

He walked over and sat on the bed. She knelt behind him, removed his jacket and began to rub his shoulders through his shirt.

"What are you going to do now?"

"Find out who did it," Clint said, "and make him pay...right after he tells me who he's working for."

THE GUNSMITH #417 - ACE HIGH

"You sound like this is personal, now, much more then just trying to help your friend keep his boat."

"When somebody tries to shoot me in the back it becomes very personal."

"Are you sure they thought it was you?"

"Ed and I were dressed alike," he said. "He pointed that out to me before he went out on deck. And there's no reason for anybody to kill him."

"What if somebody's mad that he won their money?"

He hesitated. "That could be, but it's more likely this is all connected to the sabotage."

She reached around in front of him, and slid her hands inside his shirt.

"You're very tense," she said, rubbing her hands over his bare chest. "Can I help you relax?"

"I doubt it."

He heard the nightgown slide over her skin and then saw it fly past him as she tossed it to the floor.

She kissed him on the neck, crushing her breasts against his back. He could feel her hard nipples even through his shirt.

"Well," he said, as she unbuttoned his shirt, "you could certainly try."

FORTY-FIVE

He took the time to get lost in her, figuring nobody was going to try to kill him again—at least, so soon. Still, his gun was within reach, as always.

After Adelaide massaged his muscles for a long period of time, he returned the favor. She laid down on her belly and he began to knead the flesh of her back, working his way down from her shoulders to her lower back, and then to her well-rounded buttocks. Once there, the touches became more intimate. He moved his hands down to her thighs, so that she spread her legs for him. When she did that he moved his hand between then and probed her, finding her already wet. She tensed and as he slid one finger inside of her, she gripped him. It was impressive.

"Turn over," he said.

"Massage is over?" she asked.

"Oh yeah," he said.

She turned onto her back with a smile, reached her hands up above her head and opened her legs even wider for him. He settled down on the bed between her legs and pressed his face to her. First he breathed in the scent of her, then licked the length of her pussy, tasting her thoroughly. She gasped, then laughed and reached down to touch the back of his head with one hand. He continued to work on her with his tongue and lips, also his fingers, until she was very wet. At that point he mounted her and drove himself inside her. This time her gasp was just a gasp, and she closed both of arms and legs around him as he began to pump in and out of her.

"Oh yes," she said, into his ear, "yesyesyes...don't stop..."

He had no intention of stopping. In fact, his tempo was increasing. She unwrapped her legs so she could brace her heels down on the mattress as he began to fuck her harder and harder.

"Oh Clint, yes," she said, louder now, "that's it...Oh God...that's right..."

If anybody had knocked on the door now it would have had to have been very loud, indeed. Both of them were breathing deeply, grunting at times, as the sound of their flesh slapping together filled the air. Finally, Adelaide tensed, took hold of the bedpost over her head as waves of pleasure washed over her, and in the next moment Clint let out a loud, guttural roar as he exploded inside of her...

***

"Are you relaxed now?" Adelaide asked him.
"Oh, yeah."

They were lying side-by-side, on their backs, moments later, both regaining their breath.

"Maybe now you'll be able to think more clearly."
"What?"

"It's always worked for me," she went on. "A brisk interlude of sex has always relaxed me to the point where I can think more clearly."

"You're saying I need to think about all of this more clearly?" he asked.

"We all need to think about our problems more clearly."

"Hmm," he said, staring at the ceiling. "You may have a point."

"Are you in for the night?" she asked.

"I am," he said. "There's not much we can do up on deck in the dark. I'll have to look at the scene again in the daylight."

"Then I suppose we could go to sleep?"

"I Suppose we can," he said.

And in moments, they both were...

***

In the morning, Clint rose and dressed while Adelaide was still asleep. She was lying on her stomach, her long hair off to one side, so he leaned over and kissed her on the nape of the neck before leaving the cabin.

Instead of going to breakfast, Clint went directly to the area where Ed Lockhart had been killed. He walked around, inspecting the deck. Some of Lockhart's blood was still there. He thought about having a crewman come and swab the deck clean, but then he squatted down to have a look and saw the pattern of a boot heel outlined in the blood.

He went directly to the dining room, found Henry Morgan at his table.

"Henry, I need somebody to go out on deck and cover the spot where Lockhart was killed."

"Why?"

"His blood is still there and—"

"I'll can have someone clean it."

"No," Clint said, "I don't want it cleaned, I want it protected."

"Protected?"

"So that no one will walk in it, or it won't be washed away by river water."

"But...why?"

Clint sat.

"There's a boot print in the blood."

"A boot print?"

"Specifically," Clint said, "A boot heel."

"Is there anything unusual about it?"

"Why don't you come and have a look, and maybe you can tell me?" Clint said. "Meanwhile, let's get somebody to protected it."

Henry hadn't ordered breakfast yet, so they got up and left the dining room.

***

"That boot heel," the captain said, "is not going to be any help.'

"Why not?"

"Because it will match the heel of every crew member on the boat," he said. He lifted his foot. "Including mine."

FORTY-SIX

Henry instructed Burkette to fetch an empty crate and put it down over the print.

"We'll show that to the police in Memphis," Clint said, at breakfast, "but maybe we can solve this before we get there."

"How?" Louisa asked. She had joined them earlier.

"The crew isn't allowed to eat in here, right?"

"That's right," Henry said, "there's a crew's mess."

"What have they been told about last night?"

"That there was a shooting," Henry said. "They know someone was killed, and that's all."

"Good. Why don't we bring each crew member in for a talk," Clint suggested. "We can observe their reaction when they see me, alive and well."

"You think our culprits are going to look surprised?" Louisa asked.

"I don't know," Clint said. "Maybe...concerned. I think it's worth a try, don't you?"

Henry and Louisa exchanged a glance, when Henry said, "Why not? We've tried everything else."

"What about Charlotte?" Louisa asked.

"We're still looking," Clint said. "Don't worry."

"I'm not worried," she said. "She should be worried, about me!"

"Louisa," Clint said, "in your current condition,

should you be getting so...upset?"

"No," she said, "I shouldn't, which is something else I can blame her for."

"Clint's right," Henry said. "So I'd like you to stay inside until we get to Memphis."

"Memphis?" she asked. "I thought our next stop was Greenville?"

"Clint has convinced me to skip Greenville," Henry said.

"So I'll be inside til Memphis?"

"Yes."

"But—"

"They're shooting people on deck now, Louisa," Clint said.

"They tried to shoot you," she said. "Aren't people always trying to shoot the Gunsmith?"

"Yes, but in this case," Clint said, "I think they were trying to shoot somebody who was important to the boat. They picked me because I'm looking for the saboteurs. Now, who else could they shoot that would affect the entire boat and crew?"

Louisa hesitated, then said, "Me or Henry."

"Right," Clint said. "The captain or the captain's wife. You should stay inside."

She took a deep breath, let it out, touched her belly and said, "Oh, all right."

"Good," Henry said, standing, "and I'll take you there." She stood and he took her arm. Henry looked at Clint. "I'll send Burkette to you. You and he can start questioning crew members in his cabin. All right?"

"That's fine."

Clint waved to a waiter for more coffee while Henry took his wife to their cabin.

J.R. ROBERTS

***

Clint was on his second cup with Paul Burkette appeared.

"Hello, First Mate."

"Si—Clint. The captain said you need me."

"That's right. We have work to do. Take a seat."

Burkette looked around, then sat, still not used to being in the passenger's dining room.

Clint explained his plan to Burkette, who listened intently.

"I suggest we use my men at the door. If and when you pick out one of the saboteurs, they can hold him—or her."

"That's good. Will they be armed?" Clint asked.

"Yes, we have guns on board."

"Good. We'll need two. Make it the two you trust the most."

"Aye, sir."

"I'll meet you in your cabin in...fifteen minutes?" Clint said.

"That'll do."

Clint nodded, and Burkette left.

***

Clint went back to his cabin, found Adelaide still there, dressd and reading.

"You don't seem anxious to enjoy your trip up the Mississippi," he said.

"I am enjoying it," she said, "with you, and with time for reading."

"No more poker?"

She grinned.

"That was just to meet you." She closed the Twain

collection and held it in her lap. "Are you staying?"

"No," he said, "I have things to do. I just needed to pick up something."

"What?"

He went to his saddlebag, reached it and drew out his Colt New Line.

"This," he said, showing her the little gun.

"Isn't your big gun enough?" she asked, amused.

He tucked the New Line into his belt at the small of his back.

"Someone's gunning for me," he said. "I need all the insurance I can get."

"Well then, by all means," she said. "I don't want you getting shot."

"I think it's a good idea if you remain inside," he said.

"What about supper?"

"I'll be back by then. I'll either take you to the dining room, or have it brought in here."

She held the book up and said, "So I guess I'll just keep reading."

"Good idea," he said. "It's a little dangerous out there, right now."

"More for you than anybody," she said. "Be careful."

"Always," he said, and left the cabin.

FORTY-SEVEN

Clint reached the first mate's cabin, found two men standing at the door and Burkette inside.

"This is Leland and that's Garrett. I trust them."

Clint recognized them as two of the men who had been on patrol.

"Okay," Clint said. "Let's get started."

"I'll go and get the men one by one," Burkette said.

"Starting with the ones you know or trust the least," Clint said. "Once a few men have been in here, word will get out that I'm here. Let's see if we can get this to work before that happens."

"Agreed. I'll take Garrett with me and then he'll join Leland on the door."

"That's good," Clint said. "Are you armed?"

Burkette took a derringer out of his belt. Clint was happy that he saw that both men had Colts tucked into their belts.

"All right," Clint said, "hopefully you won't need to use it."

"If I do," Burkette said, "I can put one of these bullets where it'll do the most damage."

"I'm sure you can, First Mate," Clint said.

Burkette nodded, then left the room and went down the hall with Garrett in tow, leaving Leland outside the room. Clint wondered if he should talk to the man, but decided against it. He wasn't there to make friends.

He sat at the table in the room to wait.

***

"We have a problem," Tobin said.

"I know," the other man agreed. "It's because you managed to mess everything up last night."

"How was I supposed to know it wasn't Adams on deck?" Tobin asked. "It was dark."

"Well, now he's bound and determined to find out who the saboteurs are and he's not gonna find out about me."

"What are you suggestin'?" Tobin asked. "That I give up?"

"No," the man said, "we have somebody else we can give up."

"The woman?"

"They found the dynamite in her cabin," the man said, "and they're lookin for her."

"But she's my woman."

"Then find another one," the second man said. "We either give them her, or you."

"And what about you?" Tobin asked.

"You wanna try me, Tobin?" the man asked. "Even if you kill me, our employer won't be too happy about it. Think it over. I know you'll make the right move."

The second man left, and Tobin did think it over, and caming to the only decision he could.

***

They went along as planned.

Burkette brought the men in one at a time. Clint observed their reactions when they first saw him, then he

J.R. ROBERTS

asked them a few almost meaningless questions before allowing them to leave.

After six, Clint closed the door, with Burkette on the inside.

"That's half a dozen," Clint said. "The word's bound to be out by now."

"Any of 'em look guilty?"

"Not particularly," Clint said.

"Well," Burkette said, "this wasn't a sure thing. You said it yourself."

There was a knock on the door at that point. Burkette opened it.

"Fella out here wants to talk to both of ya," Leland said.

"Send him in," Clint said.

A fortyish, thick-bodied crewman entered. He held his cap in his hand, revealing close cut grey hair.

"What are you doin' here?" Tobin demanded. He did not seem happy to see the man in the doorway.

"What's your name?" Clint asked.

"This is Tobin," Burkette said, answering the question.

"What's on your mind, Mr. Tobin?"

"The crew heard that you're lookin for a hidin' place."

"That's right."

"Well," the man said, tossing a glance at Burkette, "we got one. It's a place we made for ourselves so we can, you know, sleep and the captain and first mate can't find us."

"Is that right?" Burkette asked.

"Well," Tobin said, "the other first mate."

"Are you willing to show it to us?" Clint asked.

"Sure, I guess," the man said, worrying the cap in

195

THE GUNSMITH #417 - ACE HIGH

his hand.

"Okay," Clint said, standing up, "lead the way."

***

Tobin took them below deck, to an area Clint knew they had searched before.

"We looked down here," he said.

"Not here," Tobin said, and knocked on the wall. It sounded hollow.

"A false wall?" Clint asked.

"Yessir."

"How does it come off?"

Tobin moved to the edge of the wall, dug his fingers in and suddenly the panel popped free.

"Gimme a hand," he said, and Burkette moved in. Together they opened the wall like a door.

It revealed two things: a space large enough for a double mattress and a couple of people, and there was one person already in there.

It was Charlotte Chandler, lying on the mattress.

And she was dead.

FORTY-EIGHT

Charlotte's body was put in the same storage room as Ed Lockhart's. Clint, Henry, Louisa and Burkette were in the salon, sitting at a table with a bottle of whiskey.

Initially, Louisa was very angry, but she explained it was because she had "a lot" to say to Charlotte when she was found.

She was sitting with the men fuming with a shot glass in her hand.

Clint was quiet.

Henry and Burkette were talking, with Henry demanding to know whether or not Burkette knew about this hiding place from when he was a crewman.

"I didn't, boss," the first mate said. "I swear."

"Paul," Clint said, "why don't you talk to your men, Leland, Garrett and the others, see what they know."

"Yeah, okay," Burkette said. He looked at Henry, said, "I swear, Cap'n, I don't know," then left.

"Why are you so quiet?" Henry asked.

"Tell me about Tobin," Clint said.

"I don't know much about him," Henry admitted. "He's been with us a short time, and—"

"Did you hire him on?"

"No," Henry said, "Byron did."

"And did Byron know him?"

"No."

"Who did?" Clint asked. "Who vouched for him to Byron?"

"That would be . . " Henry was thinking.

"Burkette!" Louisa said.

"What?" Henry said.

"It was Burkette," Louisa said.

"How do you know that?" Clint asked.

"I do the paperwork, remember?" she said. "When he signed on, I knew who recommended him and who hired him." She looked at Henry.

"Burkette wasn't on your list, was he, Louisa?" Clint asked. "You never trusted him."

"No," she said. "I didn't."

"But Henry did."

"Yes," she said, "but Henry wants to trust everyone, Clint. He's loyal, and he thinks everybody is. This has been very hard for him."

"So I've been stupid," Henry said.

"Not stupid, Henry," Clint said. "Loyal."

"Stupidly loyal," Henry said. "So what are you sayin'?"

"Tobin and Burkette took me right to that hiding place," Clint said.

"You think they're working together?" Henry asked. "They're the saboteurs?"

"And they killed Charlotte?" Louisa asked.

"So we'd stop looking for her," Clint said.

"So by making Burkette first mate, I made sure we wouldn't find his partners," Henry said.

"You're being too hard on yourself, Henry," Clint said.

"So what will you do?" Louisa asked.

"Burkette was careful not to bring Tobin to me,"

J.R. ROBERTS

Clint said. "The mate didn't look happy to see him when he walked in."

"You don't think Burkette knew he was comin'?" Henry asked.

"Maybe not," Clint said. "Henry, have we bypassed Greenville yet?"

"We have," Henry said. "We're on our way to Memphis."

"Okay," Clint said, "then let's get this settled before Memphis."

"How?" Henry asked.

"If Burkette and Tobin are working together," Clint said, "we have to split them apart. Pit them against each other."

"Tell me how we do that," Henry said.

"You won't like it," Clint said.

"Why not?"

"Because," Clint said, "I want to use Louisa."

"Me?"

"Why?" Henry asked.

"Because they'll believe her."

"About what?" Henry asked.

"About anything," Clint said. "I mean, look at her. Who would believe she's a liar?"

Both men looked at Louisa, who simply stared back.

"Okay," Henry said, "so explain."

***

It took him only a few minutes to explain his plan.

"That seems too simple," Louisa said.

"Too simple to work," Henry said.

"When it comes to beautiful women," Clint said, "men are gullible. Look what Charlotte did to me. She got me to bring her and her dynamite on board."

"You can't blame yourself for that," Louisa said.

"Henry," Clint said, "your wife is a beautiful woman. She's going to have to sell this to Burkette and Tobin."

"I'm afraid Louisa is not a very good liar," Henry said, sadly.

Clint smiled. "Do you really believe that?"

"Of course," Henry said. "She's never lied to me." He looked at his wife. "Have you?"

"Of course not, darling." She smiled at Clint.

"What are you two grinnin' at?" Henry asked.

"Tell me what to do, Clint," Louisa said, "and who to do it to."

"I'm thinking Burkette first," Clint said. "He'll be the one you can get to, and the easiest."

"All right."

"And then Tobin. We'll get the two of you in the same place, somehow."

"I can work on that," Henry said.

"Good," Clint said, "then you get her together with Tobin, and I'll get her together with Burkette, and...we'll see."

FORTY-NINE

When the first knock came at the door, Louisa's heart leaped. She calmed herself and called out, "Come in."

The door opened and first mate Burkette entered.

"Ma'am," he said, "Clint said you need to see me?"

"Yes, First Mate, I do. Please, close the door and sit."

"Ma'am?"

"Please, sit."

"Ma'am, you're the captain's wife."

"Does that mean you can't sit?"

"I should leave the door open."

"Very well," she said. "Do it."

"Yes, Ma'am."

He moved away from the open door and sat down across the table from her.

"First Mate, how well do you know a man named Tobin?"

"He's one of the crew."

She touched the papers on the table.

"According to my records, you're the one who recommended to Byron Stanhope that he hire him."

"That may be," Burkette said, looking perfectly calm. "I don't really remember."

"Well, he remembers you," she said. "He's told the Captain that you have been sabotaging the Natchez

Queen."

"What?" he said. "That can't be." He no longer looked calm. "How do you know?"

"I heard the captain telling Clint," she said.

He narrowed his eyes. "And why are you tellin' me?"

"The Captain asked me to," she said. "He trusts you. That's why he named you first mate. And if he trusts you, I trust you."

He hesitated, then said, "I appreciate that."

Clint and Henry had warned her that Burkette might take some time to decide whether he believed her or not. Henry had wanted to hide in the other room, but Clint didn't think that was a good idea.

She had a derringer, which she holding within the folds of her dress. If he made a menacing move toward her, she would shoot him. Henry did not think she'd be able to do it, but Clint did. He also knew that all wives lie to their husbands on occasion, about something.

"I think," she said, "Tobin has been sabotaging our boat, and he's trying to blame you."

"That seems right."

"He had an accomplice," she said, "a woman named Charlotte. He killed her. He also killed Ed Lockhart, mistaking him for Clint, in the dark."

"What do you want me to do, Ma'am?" Burkette asked.

"I don't know, First Mate," she said. "I'm just... warning you."

He stood up. She gripped the derringer more tightly.

"Thank you, Ma'am," he said. "I'll take care of it."

She nodded. He turned and left, closing the door behind him.

***

When the door opened again it was her husband, Henry.

"Come," he said, holding his hand out to her. "It's time for step two."

She rose, took his hand and followed.

***

"Ma'am?"

Louisa turned, saw Tobin looking at her. They were on deck.

"Mr. Tobin."

"The Captain said you needed help with somethin'?"

"That's right," she said. "A crate. I need it to be brought to my cabin. It's below."

"If you tell me where it is," he said, "I'll gladly fetch it for you."

"It looks like any other crate, I'm afraid," she said. "But I can show you which one it is, if you'll come below with me."

"Just the two of us?" he asked. "Ma'am...you're the Captain's wife."

"And that's why you'll help me," she said, "isn't it?"

"Yes, Ma'am."

***

Below deck Clint and Henry waited among the crates and cargo.

"I don't like this," Henry said. "Louisa could get hurt. The baby..."

"We're both here," Clint said, "and she has a gun. We'll make sure nothing happens to her."

"It better not."

***

THE GUNSMITH #417 - ACE HIGH

When Louisa and Tobin got down to the hold of the boat, Tobin asked, "Okay, Ma'am, which one is it."

"Mr. Tobin," she said, "did you know First Mate Burkette before you came aboard?"

"What? Um, why?"

"Well, my records show that he was the one who recommended to First Mate Stanhope that he hire you."

"I believe we did meet before. If he did that, I owe him a debt."

"That's strange," she said.

"What is?"

"Well," she said, "my husband seems to think Burkette is the saboteur who's been damaging the ship and killing people."

"I, uh, wouldn't know anything about that."

"But Burkette says it's you."

"What?" Tobin looked shocked.

"Yes, he told the Captain you killed Lockhart, and the woman, and set the dynamite."

"That sonofa—" Tobin stopped short. "Why are you tellin' me all this?"

"Because I'd hate to see an innocent member of the crew take the blame for this," Louisa said.

"Swell," Tobin said, "thanks, but can tell you it ain't me, it's him." He turned to leave.

"Hey!" she yelled. "How about my crate!"

"Sorry, Ma'am!" Tobin called, and was gone.

Louisa turned and said, "Henry?"

"We're here." Henry and Clint stepped out from hiding. Louisa rushed to her husband, who hugged her. "You did great."

"What now?" she asked.

"Now," Clint said, "we keep them from killing each other."

"Why?" she asked. "Why not let them kill each other and be done with it?"

"Because we need them to implicate each other," Clint said.

"Well," Henry said, "there's no place else on board to hide, so let's go get 'em. Louisa, you go back to the cabin and lock yourself in."

"No," Clint said, "go to the bridge and stay with the pilot." Clint looked at Henry. "You trust him, right?"

"Implicitly." He looked at Louisa. "Tell Andy I said he should keep you safe."

"Okay," Louisa said. "And you two keep yourselves safe."

"That's what we'll do," Clint said, "as soon as we all get out of here."

FIFTY

They didn't have far to look.

Burkette and Tobin had come together up on deck. There were some other crewman surrounding them. Clint and Henry Morgan joined the circle.

Both men were armed, waving their guns around as they faced each other.

"You gave me up you, you sonofabitch!" Tobin shouted at Burkette.

"Shut up, Tobin!" Burkette said. "I never said a word, and now you're givin' me up. Don't you see what they're doin'?"

"I see you made me kill Charlotte to cover for you, and now you wanna give me to them," Tobin said. "It ain't gonna happen."

Burkette looked around, saw Clint and Henry standing with the rest of the crew.

"Look," he said to Tobin, pointing. "They set us up!"

Both men turned to face Clint and Henry. They already had their guns in their hands. Henry had a gun tucked into his belt, and Clint's was holstered. Suddenly, the other crewmen broke their circle and crowded off to one side.

"You're so smart," Burkette said. "How smart can you be when you made me first mate, huh?"

"You're right, Paul," Henry said. "I'm not so smart.

THE GUNSMITH #417 - ACE HIGH

But neither are you. You're facin' the deadliest gunman the West has ever seen."

"Ha!" Tobin said. "We got our guns in our hands, already. We can take 'im, Burkette."

"We need to know who the two of you are working for," Clint said. "Who ordered all the sabotage to the Natchez Queen so they'd be able to buy it out from under Captain Morgan. You tell us that and I won't kill you."

"Listen to him," Tobin said. "He believes his own legend."

Tobin seemed intent on standing his ground, but Burkette didn't seem so sure.

"The game is up, Burkette," Clint said. "You're smart enough to see that. Everybody here has already heard the truth."

Burkette and Tobin were holding their guns at their sides. Clint was ready for either one to raise their weapon.

"Clint..." Henry said, his own hand hovering near his gun.

"Stand fast, Captain," Clint said. "I've got this."

Henry lowered his hand. After all, this was part of the reason he'd asked Clint to come.

"Burkette," Clint said, "make the smart choice."

"Yeah, Burkette," Tobin said, "Make the smart choice. Kill him!"

He started to bring his gun up. Clint drew and in one quick motion fired, sending a bullet right into Tobin's chest. The man's mouth opened in shock, the gun fell from his hand, and he slumped to the deck.

Before he fell, Burkette dropped his gun and shouted, "Hey, wait, wait!" and put his hands out in front of him to ward off any bullets.

"Smart move," Clint said. "Henry, he's all yours. Lock him up someplace, until we get to Memphis."

J.R. ROBERTS

Henry looked around, said "Leland, Garrett, take him! Let's go!"

"Before you do that," Clint said, "does anyone else want to step forward?"

The men looked puzzled.

"Was anyone else working with these two?"

A rumble went through the crew as they started looking at each other.

"Just remember what happened here today," Clint said. "If you were working with them, get off in Memphis and never come back."

"Everybody, back to work now!" Henry shouted. "Leland, Garrett, take him!"

The two men stepped forward and each took one of Burkette's arms.

***

When they pulled into dock in Memphis, Adelaide Buckley was on deck with Clint.

"Where are you off to now?" she asked.

"I'll stay with the Natchez Queen a while longer," he said. "Make sure the boat's fortunes have changed."

"You think they will? Because you're playing poker here?"

"Maybe not because of that."

"What, then?"

"There was a gunfight on deck," Clint said. "Gunfights have ways of making towns famous. Maybe it will do the same for the Queen."

"Lucky Queen."

"Why don't you stay a while longer?"

"I wish I could," she said, touching his arm. "I have things to do, places to be. Maybe we'll run into each

THE GUNSMITH #417 - ACE HIGH

other again."

"That would be nice."

She kissed his cheek and moved toward the gangplank.

***

The police came on board and removed Paul Burkette. Henry Morgan went with them, returning a few hours later. He found Clint sitting at his poker table in the salon.

"Well, that's over," he said, sitting opposite him. "Burkette gave up Everett Winston. Apparently, he *is* the kind of businessman who hires thugs to help him get what he wants."

"You're going to need another dealer," Clint said, "to replace Lockhart."

"I know," Henry said, "maybe even a good one, this time."

"I can make some recommendations."

"That would be good. And you'll stay on?"

"For a while," Clint said. "At least until we find out if the gunfight attracts passengers."

"'Take a ride on a riverboat where the Gunsmith showed his talent with a gun,'" Henry said. "Something like that?"

Clint made a face and told his friend, "Let's work on it."

ABOUT THE AUTHOR

As "J.R. Roberts" Bob Randisi is the creator and author of the long running western series, *The Gunsmith*. Under various other pseudonyms he has created and written the "Tracker," "Mountain Jack Pike," "Angel Eyes," "Ryder," "Talbot Roper," "The Son of Daniel Shaye," and "the Gamblers" Western series. His western short story collection, *The Cast-Iron Star and Other Western Stories*, is now available in print and as an ebook from Western Fictioneers Books.

In the mystery genre he is the author of the *Miles Jacoby*, *Nick Delvecchio*, *Gil & Claire Hunt*, *Dennis McQueen*, *Joe Keough*, and *The Rat Pack*, series. He has written more than 500 western novels and has worked in the Western, Mystery, Sci-Fi, Horror and Spy genres. He is the editor of over 30 anthologies. All told he is the author of over 650 novels. His arms are very, very tired.

He is the founder of the Private Eye Writers of America, the creator of the Shamus Award, the co-founder of Mystery Scene Magazine, the American Crime Writers League, Western Fictioneers and their Peacemaker Award.

In 2009 the Private Eye Writers of America awarded him the Life Achievement Award, and in 2013 the Readwest Foundation presented him with their President's Award for Life Achievement.

PRO SE PRODUCTIONS PRESENTS

A NEW PULP COLLECTION OF HISTORIC PROPORTIONS!

Yesterday's Style, Today's Best Writers.

Heroes for Tomorrow.

BLACK PULP is a wonderful anthology of short stories that expands the world of Tarzan, Doc Savage, The Avenger, The Shadow, The Spider, The Phantom Detective, The Green Lama, Ki-Gor, G-8, Secret Agent X, Secret Service Operator #5, and their contemporaries. And BLACK PULP populates this world with hitmen, boxers-turned-vigilantes, female aviators, wildmen, mercenaries-for-hire, private detectives, femme fatales, naval aviators, freedom-fighting pirates, paranormal investigators, real life lawmen, adventurers, and many more.

– Lucas Garrett, Reviewer, Pulp Fiction Reviews

> Strictly adult, with a stress on a fictional world where heroes of color take center stage, readers will love these yarns of mayhem and mischief, of right hooks and upper cuts, war tales, pirates, and sleuths looking for clues among stiffs....Here, Black Pulp is gathered from the very best of the New Pulp scribes, with a genius for action and romance, drawing from the fantastic, grotesque, and magical. Read and become bewitched.
>
> – Robert Fleming, www.aalbc.com

Pulp fiction, in many cases, is the second movement in the dialectic of inner transition. It is the antithesis of what is expected and the stepping stone to true freedom.

– Best Selling Author Walter Mosley, from his introduction to BLACK PULP

PRO SE PRESS

Available at amazon.com and other fine outlets. Pro Se Productions www.prose-press.com

THE NEW ADVENTURES OF
FOSTER FADE
THE CRIME SPECTACULARIST
FEATURING CHARACTERS CREATED BY LESTER DENT
With Stories by
Adam Lance GARCIA
Derrick FERGUSON
Aubrey STEPHENS
David WHITE
H. David BLALOCK
WHITE HOT CORPSES!
THE CRIME SPECTAC
MIKE FYLES
PRO SE PRESS
PULP OBSCURA
PULP OBSCURA IS AN IMPRINT OF PRO SE PRODUCTIONS AND IS PUBLISHED IN CONJUNCTION WITH TITLES FROM ALTUS PRESS.
AVAILABLE AT AMAZON.COM AND WWW.PROSE-PRESS.COM

CPSIA information can be obtained
at www.ICGtesting.com
Printed in the USA
LVOW13s1722020418
571981LV00013B/176/P